HEARTS AT STAKE

THE DRAKE CHRONICLES

ALYXANDRA HARVEY

Walker & Company ✹ New York

First published in the United States of America in January 2010
by Walker Publishing Company, Inc.
A division of Bloomsbury Publishing, Inc.
Visit Walker & Company's Web site at www.bloomsburyteens.com

For information about permission to reproduce selections from this book, write to
Permissions, Walker & Company, 175 Fifth Avenue, New York, New York 10010

Library of Congress Cataloging-in-Publication Data
Harvey, Alyxandra.
Hearts at stake / by Alyxandra Harvey. — 1st U.S. ed.
p.   cm.
Summary: As her momentous sixteenth birthday approaches, Solange Drake, the only
born female vampire in 900 years, is protected by her large family of brothers and her
human best friend Lucy from increasingly persistent attempts on her life by the powerful vampire
queen and her followers.
ISBN 978-0-8027-2074-0 (paperback) • ISBN 978-0-8027-9840-4 (hardcover)
[1. Vampires—Fiction. 2. Interpersonal relations—Fiction. 3. Brothers and sisters—
Fiction. 4. Friendship—Fiction.] I. Title.
PZ7.H267448He 2010   [Fic]—dc22   2009023156

Book design by Danielle Delaney
Typeset by Westchester Book Composition
Printed in the U.S.A. by Quebecor World Fairfield, Pennsylvania
2 4 6 8 10 9 7 5 3 1 (paperback)
2 4 6 8 10 9 7 5 3 1 (hardcover)

All papers used by Walker & Company are natural, recyclable products
made from wood grown in well-managed forests. The manufacturing processes
conform to the environmental regulations of the country of origin.

Thanks and chocolate kisses to:

♦ My editor, Emily Easton, and everyone at Walker Books/Bloomsbury, known and unknown, who have helped make this book a reality. You are the cause of many happy dances in my kitchen.

♦ My wonderful agent, Marlene Stringer, who is helping to make my dreams come true.

♦ My parents, who are unfailingly supportive and love me just the way I am, tattoos, pink hair, and all.

♦ My long-time BFF Jess, Google Queen Extraordinaire, for the cheerleading, commiserating, and demands for more books.

♦ My husband, Khayman, who guards my writing time almost as zealously as I do, and who only ever wants me to be me.

♦ All my friends and family, especially Crystal, who regularly drives all the way up to the farmhouse for visits.

PROLOGUE

◆

Lucy

Friday, early evening

Normally I wouldn't have been caught dead at a field party.

If you'll pardon the pun.

This was a supreme sacrifice on my part for my best friend, Solange, who was having a really bad day, which was about to turn into a *really* bad week. Her sixteenth birthday was coming up, and we weren't talking a new car and a pink dress for her sweet sixteen. Not in her family.

This wasn't much better though.

She was standing in the middle of a field, trying to drink cheap wine and pretend she didn't want to be anywhere but here. The music was passable but that was about all it had to recommend it. The cars were parked in a wide circle, the sun setting behind the trees with all the colors of a blood orange pulled into pieces. Practically my entire high school was here; there wasn't much else to do on one of the last weekends before school started. People danced and flirted in a sea of baseball caps and faded denim. Someone burped loudly.

"This was *such* a bad idea," I muttered.

Solange smiled softly, abandoning her plastic cup on the hood of someone's rusted truck.

"It was a nice thought."

"It was stupid," I admitted. She just looked so sad lately, I'd hoped a complete change of pace might distract her from all that worrying. Instead it made me want to bare my pitifully human teeth at the rowdies. Someone's shoe nudged my heel, and when I looked back at it, I was greeted with way too much information about the mating habits of my fellow students. I kicked hard at the boot.

"No one needs to see that," I said, turning away quickly before more clothing came off. The couple giggled and went deeper into the corn. I stared at Solange. "What the hell was I thinking?"

She half grinned.

"It is rather unlike you."

Darren, from my math class last year, tripped over his own feet and sprawled in the dirt in front of us before I could answer. His grin was sloppy. He was nice enough usually; in fact, he was the reason I hadn't entirely flunked out of math. But he was drunk and desperate to fit in.

"Hi, Lucy." Apparently beer made him lisp. My name came out as "Loothee"—which was marginally better than my real name, which was Lucky. I had *those* kind of parents, but I'd made everyone at school call me Lucy since the first day of first grade.

"Hi, Darren."

He blinked at Solange. Even in jeans and a tank top she looked dramatic. It was all that pale skin and those pale eyes. Her black bangs were choppy because she trimmed them herself. The rest was long and hung past her shoulders. Mine was plain old brown and cut in a wedged bob to my chin. My glasses were retro—dark rimmed and vaguely cat's-eye shaped. I didn't need them to see the way Darren was drooling over Solange. All guys drooled over her. She was beautiful, end of discussion.

"Who's your friend? She's hot."

"You've met her before." Solange was homeschooled, but I dragged her around when I could. "Sober up, Darren. This isn't a good look for you."

"'Kay." He spat grass out of his mouth.

I slung my arm through hers. "Let's get out of here. The sun's starting to set anyway, and maybe we can salvage the rest of the night."

The wind was soft through the corn, rustling the stalks as we wandered away. The stars were starting to peek out, like animal eyes in the dark. We could still hear the music and the occasional shout of laughter. Twilight was starting to settle like a soft blue veil. We'd walked from my house, which was a half hour away. We'd probably waited too long. We picked up our pace.

And then Solange paused.

"What?" I froze beside her, my shoulders tensing until I was practically wearing them as earmuffs. I was all too aware of what could be out there. I should never have suggested this. I'd just put her into even more danger. I was an idiot.

She held up her hand, her eyes so pale suddenly that they were nearly colorless, a ring of ice around a black lake. And because I was scared, I scowled into the gathering shadows around us. Mom always said bravado was a karmic debt I had to work through. She was basically saying I'd been mouthy and obnoxious for several lifetimes now. But somehow I didn't think this particular situation called for a round of *oms*, which was my mother's favorite way of cleansing karmic baggage. Most babies were sung lullabies; I got "Om Namah Shivaya" when I was really fussy.

"Cops?" I suggested, mostly because they seemed like the better alternative. "They always break up these parties."

She shook her head. She looked delicate and ethereal, as if she were made of lily petals. Few people knew the marble all that softness concealed.

"They're close," she murmured. "Watching."

"Run?" I suggested. "Like, right now?"

She shook her head again, but we did at least start walking.

"If we act like prey, they'll act like predators."

I tried not to hyperventilate, tried to walk quickly but confidently, as if we weren't being stalked. Sometimes I really hated Solange's life. It was totally unfair.

"You're getting angry," she said softly.

"Damn right I am. Those undead bastards think they can do this to you just because—"

"When you're angry, your heart beats faster. It's like the cherry on a hot fudge sundae."

"Oh. Right." I always forgot that little detail. Maybe my mom was right. I needed to take up meditating.

"Lucy, I want you to run."

"Shut up," I said, disbelief making my voice squeaky.

"They'll follow me if I run in the opposite direction."

"That's the worst plan I've ever heard," I grumbled, fighting the urge to look over my shoulder. Stupid creepy cornfields. Stupid creepy stalkers. A cricket sang suddenly from the tall corn and my heart nearly shot straight out of my chest. I actually pressed my hand against my rib cage, half-worried. The cricket went quiet and was replaced by the rumble of car tires on the ground. Cornstalks snapped. A familiar jeep skidded to a dusty halt in front of us.

"Nicholas," Solange breathed, relieved.

"Get in," he snapped.

I was slightly less enamored with her older brother, but I had to admit he had good timing. In his black shirt and dark hair, he blended into the night. Only his eyes gave him away, silver and fierce. He was gorgeous, there was no use in denying it, but he always knew just how to make me want to poke him in the eye with a fork.

Like right now.

"Drive," he said to their brother Logan, who was behind the steering wheel. He didn't even wait for me to get in. Logan lifted his foot off the brake. The car rolled forward.

"Hey!" I shouted.

"Nicholas Drake, you let her in the car right now." Solange leaned forward between the front seats.

"She's fine. We have to get you out of here."

I grabbed on to the half-opened window. Logan slowed down.

"Sorry, Lucy, I thought you were in already," he said.

"Don't you *read?*" I asked Nicholas, disgusted. "If you leave me here now that you've got Solange all safe, they'll grab me to get to her."

Solange opened the back door and I leaped in. The car sped off. Shadows flitted beside us, menacing, hungry. I shivered. Then I smacked the back of Nicholas's head.

"Idiot."

CHAPTER 1

◆

Solange

"I can't believe you were actually going to just leave her there," I grumbled again as Logan pulled into our lane, which was overgrown with hedges. The unnatural glint of unnatural eyes had faded, and there was nothing but ripe blackberries and crickets in the bushes. Not only was our farm well protected, but it was also surrounded by other family farms, with forest surrounding all of them. Drakes have lived in this area since it was considered wild and dangerous, best left to gunslingers and outlaws. Now it was just home.

But dangerous all the same.

"She was fine," Nicholas said testily. "She was safe as soon as we got you away from her." He only ever called her "she," except to her face, when he called her Lucky because it annoyed her so much. They'd been getting on each other's nerves since we were kids. There was a family joke that Lucy's first words were, "Nicholas is bugging me." I couldn't remember ever *not* knowing her. She'd drawn me out of my shell, even when we were little, though it wasn't until my fifth birthday that I'd started calling her my best friend, after she threw a mud ball at Nicholas's head for stealing my chocolate cupcake. We'd learned to ride bikes together and liked the same movies and talked all night whenever we had slumber parties.

"She was *fine*," Nicholas insisted, catching my glare. "Despite being reckless."

"She was just trying to help me."

"She's *human*," he said, as if it were a debilitating disease, as if he wasn't human as well, despite the bloodchange. We aren't undead, like the horror novels say, though we definitely look it during our transformation. That particular stereotype clings so deeply that sometimes it's easier to embrace it. Lucy's mom calls us "differently abled."

"And you're a jerk." I touched his sleeve. "But thanks for coming to get me."

"You're welcome," he muttered. "You know you shouldn't let her talk you into stuff. It never turns out well."

"I know. But you know how Lucy is. And she meant well."

He grunted. Logan grinned.

"She's getting cuter. Especially from behind."

"She is *not*," Nicholas said. "And quit looking at her butt."

I was so totally going to tell Lucy they'd been talking about her butt.

"You're such an old man," Logan said scornfully, turning off the ignition. "We have all this power. We should use it."

"Flirting is not a power," I told him drily.

"It is if you're good at it. And I'm *very* good at it."

"So you keep telling us."

"Being charming's my gift," he said modestly. No one else could have pulled off such an old-fashioned shirt with lace cuffs and such a pretty face. The pheromones that vampires emit like a dangerous perfume keep humans enticed and befuddled with longing, and Logan's are especially well tuned. They don't have an actual smell that can be described, except lately in my case. It's more subliminal than that, with the power to hypnotize. Kind of like the way wild animals can smell each other out in the forest, especially during mating season. If a vampire is particularly strong, humans don't even remember being a meal; they just have a craving for rare steak or spinach. If we drink too much, they become anemic.

The pheromones don't work on other vampires, except, of course, for mine, which are rapidly becoming a beacon for all of vampire kind. I'm special, and not in a good way, if you ask me. Vampires are rarely born, except in certain ancient families ... Exhibit A, me and my seven obnoxious older brothers.

But I'm the only girl.

In about nine hundred years.

And the closer I get to my sixteenth birthday, the more I attract the others to me. It's all very Snow White, except I don't call bluebirds and deer out of the woods—only bloodthirsty vampires who want to kidnap me or kill me. Vampire politics are messy at best, and all Drakes have been exiled from the royal court since the very hour I was born. I'm considered a threat to the current ruler, Lady Natasha, because my genealogy is so impressive and because there's some stupid prophecy from centuries ago that says the vampire tribes will be properly united under the rule of a daughter born to an ancient family.

And Lady Natasha, unlike me, wasn't born into an ancient family—even if she considers herself to be the reigning vampire queen.

As if that's my fault.

Luckily, my family much prefers living in quiet exile in the woods. I'd heard enough rumors about our ruler to be glad we'd never actually met. She feeds off humans and is barely circumspect about it; in fact, she loves the attention and the vampire groupies. She apparently doesn't like pretty young girls; they never seem to survive her mood swings.

Technically, she shouldn't be feeding off humans, and certainly not so nonchalantly. It was becoming an issue, even among her own people. There are royalists who follow her just because she's so powerful, not because they particularly respect her. Fear, as always, is a great motivator.

And lately she's been turning more and more humans into vampires, in order to gather more followers. The council makes her nervous, and I make her nervous, but most of all Leander Montmartre makes her nervous.

He has that affect on all of us.

He's been turning humans for nearly three hundred years now, and he's so violent and careless about it, he's basically created a new breed of vampire. He leaves them half-turned and usually buried under the ground, to conquer the bloodchange on their own without any help at all. The thirst is so strong that it twists them and gives them a double set of fangs instead of just our one retractable pair. The ones that stay loyal to Montmartre are called the Host. The ones who defect call themselves the Cwn Mamau, the Hounds of the Mothers. They were either strong enough to survive alone, or were rescued and trained by other Hounds. Everyone knew they wanted to kill Montmartre, but they were so reclusive they wouldn't accept outside help. They are fiercely independent, live in caves, serve a shamanka (female shaman), and wear bone beads in their hair. They're kind of scary, but nowhere near as scary as the most dangerous of Montmartre's creations called the *Hel-Blar*, who have blue-tinted skin, and teeth that are all fangs, sharpened like needles and unretractable. *Hel-Blar* means "blue death" in some ancient Viking language. Their bite, known as a "kiss," can infect without any blood exchange, and it's rumored they can turn both vampires and humans into *Hel-Blar*. Even Montmartre avoids them as much as possible. He's not big on cleaning up his own mess. And they want him dead even more than the Hounds do—when they're lucid enough to want anything more than blood. The Host and the Hounds managed to stay sane, unlike the *Hel-Blar*. No one can control them, not even Montmartre.

We live peacefully with other humans, and our family is one of the few ancient clans of the Raktapa Council. The council was formed ages ago when the families realized that we weren't like other vampires: our change is genetic. We transform without being bitten, but we need vampire blood to survive that transformation. Afterward, we're nearly immortal, like the others, vulnerable only to a stake through the heart, too much sunlight, or decapitation.

"Do Mom and Dad know about what happened after the party?" I asked, finally getting out of the car and facing the house. The original building had burned down during the Salem witch trials, even though we were nowhere near Salem. The locals had been superstitious and scared of every little thing. The house was rebuilt farther into the sheltering forest. It was simple and a little shabby from the outside, but the pioneer-style log cabin hid a luxurious heart full of velvet couches and stone fireplaces. The rosebushes under the leaded-glass windows were a little scraggly, the oak trees old and stately. I loved every single treated inch of it. Even my mother's pinched and disapproving face behind the glass.

"Busted," Logan murmured.

Moths flung themselves at the lamps. The screen door creaked when I pushed it open.

"Solange Rosamund Drake."

I winced. Behind me, both my brothers did the same. My mother, Helena, was intimidating at the best of times with her long black hair and her pale eyes, and the fact that she can take down someone twice her size with a sword, a stake, or her petite bare hands.

"Ouch—middle name." Logan shot me a sympathetic smile before easing into the living room and out of the crossfire.

"Snitch." I pinched Nicholas. He only raised an eyebrow.

"Nicholas didn't tell us anything." My mom pinned him with a pointed glare. He squirmed a little. I'd known grown men to back away physically from that look. "One of your aunts was patrolling the perimeter and saw your escape."

"Escape." I rolled my eyes. "It was barely anything. They didn't even come out of the cornfields. They were just sniffing me."

"You have to be more careful," my father, Liam, said calmly from his favorite chair. It kind of looked like a medieval throne. No surprise there. He'd only been born in 1901 but he carried himself like a king.

"I feel fine," I said, exasperated. He was drinking brandy. I could smell it across the room, just like I could smell Uncle Geoffrey's cologne, Aunt Hyacinth's pug, and the thick perfume of roses. Just another one of our little gifts. I rubbed my nose so I wouldn't sneeze.

"What's with all the flowers?" I asked, noticing the roses. There were dozens and dozens of them everywhere, in every shade of red, stuffed in crystal vases, teacups, and jam jars.

"From your . . . admirers," my father told me grimly.

"What?" Admirers, ha! They were only coming around because of my pheromones. It's not my fault I smell funny. I shower every day, but apparently I still stink of lilies and warm chocolate and something else no one can accurately describe. Even Lucy commented on it once, and she's nearly immune to us, having practically grown up here. No one else was smelly in such an obvious way; pheromones are usually subtle and mysterious. I really hope it fades once I fully turn.

The prophecy and my family's legacy in the vampire world won't, though.

Sometimes it sucks having a family that's so old and powerful.

"Darling, it's a great compliment, I'm sure," my aunt Hyacinth said. She was technically my great-great-great-aunt. She didn't look much over forty, even though she clung to the fashions of her youth in the privacy of the tribe, like most vampires. Her dress was Victorian in style, with a lace corset and jet beads. "When I was your age I had the best time. There's nothing like the rush of being a debutante. All those men hungering after you." She gave a delicate shiver.

"Hyacinth." Dad grimaced. "You hadn't even been turned then, and this is hardly a debutante's ball. They don't want to waltz, damn it." My great-great-great-uncle Edward had married Aunt Hyacinth in 1853 and turned her in 1877, at her insistence. She was inspired by Queen Victoria's undying love for her own husband and wanted to live for centuries by Edward's side. I'd never met him, though, because he'd died in World War I, shot one night on a spy mission for the Allies because he was determined to do his part. She'd been alone ever since.

I glanced at a thick cream-colored paper card pinned to an enormous bouquet of white roses in a red box and froze.

"Montmartre?" I squeaked. "He sent me flowers?"

Dad flicked the box a baleful glare. "Yes."

"I'm putting them down the incinerator," I said darkly. The last thing I wanted was Montmartre or his Host to know who I was. I was also hoping to slip out while everyone else was distracted. I should have known better.

"You can do that later." Mom pointed to a chair. "Sit."

I dropped onto a velvet settee. Nicholas sat as well, joining my other brothers, who were all watching me grimly.

"Don't you lot have anything better to do?" I asked.

"Than protecting our annoying baby sister?" Quinn drawled. "No."

Being the only girl in a family of boys would have been tough enough to navigate, never mind a family with the rare ability to give birth to mostly male vampires. Even among the Drakes, that ability is rare. Most vampires are "made," not born. My mom, for example, had been human until my dad turned her shortly after I was born and they'd decided they didn't want any more children. He'd been born human too, like my brothers, until his sixteenth birthday—when he'd sickened, the way we all did—and would have died if my aunt hadn't given him her blood to drink.

Family legend has it that the first of our clan was William Drake. No one knows how he was turned. We did know he married Veronique DuBois, a lady-in-waiting to Queen Eleanor of Aquitaine. A year after their wedding, she went into labor with their firstborn. After twenty-seven hours of childbirth, the midwife told William that Veronique was not going to survive the birth. In desperation, William turned her, and their twins were born healthy. By their sixteenth birthday, though, the twins weakened and grew unnaturally sensitive to the sunlight. They were hungry but couldn't eat, thirsty but couldn't drink. Nothing tempted them.

Except blood.

And so the Drake vampire family began.

Veronique, as the oldest surviving Drake, is our family matriarch. William was staked by a hunter during the reign of Henry VIII. Veronique rarely visited, preferring to have us come to her once we'd survived the change and she could afford to get attached. At least she hadn't joined us tonight, which meant it wasn't a formal meeting, just a family ambush. She was scary enough that she probably could have given Lady Natasha a run for her crown if she'd wanted it. Luckily for everyone, she preferred embroidery to court intrigue.

"Solange, are you listening to me?"

I jerked my head up.

"Yes." I'd heard this particular lecture enough times over the last few months to know it intimately. "Nothing happened. You're all overreacting." I did feel guilty; I just knew better than to show it.

"There were at least three of them in that field tonight, maybe more." Nicholas scowled. "You know they don't all send flowers. Most of them just want to grab you and run."

I scowled back. "I could have handled it. It wasn't even full dark yet. Besides, if they were so dangerous, why'd you nearly leave Lucy behind?"

"You were going to leave Lucy there?" my mom sputtered, and Nicholas narrowed his eyes at me. I crossed my eyes smugly. Growing up with so many brothers taught me the fine art of misdirection, self-preservation, and revenge, if nothing else.

"She was *fine*." I knew Nicholas was trying not to slump in his chair. "They weren't after her. And she's not fragile, for God's sake."

"She's under the protection of this family," my father said.

"I know, but she can look after herself. Broke my nose last summer, didn't she?"

"Be that as it may."

"Okay, okay." Nicholas backed down.

"And you, young lady." Dad turned to me. Every single one of my traitor brothers smirked. They look enough alike that people usually assume they're all sets of twins. Only Quinn and Connor are actually twins. Quinn keeps his hair long and Connor, like Sebastian, prefers to fade quietly into the background. Logan is the flamboyant one, and Nicholas spends most of his free time worrying about me. Marcus and Duncan just came home from a road trip. They're all gorgeous; it's like living with a bunch of male models. And it makes girls stupid around them.

"You have to take this seriously."

"I do, Dad," I said quietly. "You know I do."

"What I know is that they're coming for you and soon you'll be weaker than a blind kitten."

"I know." This totally sucked. I was getting in trouble over a party I hadn't wanted to go to in the first place. I *like* being alone and staying on the farm. But I hate being trapped and hovered over.

"Let the girl be," Hyacinth said, drinking delicately from a goblet. It looked like cherry cordial. It wasn't.

"Thank you." I swallowed thickly.

Did I mention?

I was squeamish about blood.

CHAPTER 2

◆

Lucy

"Lucy, is that you?"

I kicked the door shut with my heel, still muttering under my breath. Nicholas was so infuriating. What was wrong with him anyway?

"Lucy?"

"Yeah, it's me," I called out.

"Where have you been? We nearly started without you, kiddo." Dad came out of the kitchen with a bowl of hot popcorn, made from the corn he'd grown in the backyard. It was as close to junk food as my parents came. His long hair was in its usual ponytail, his sleeves rolled up to display his wolf and turtle tattoos. The wolf was his personal totem, and the turtle was our family totem.

"Pick out a movie, honey." Mom looked up from the beads spread out on the coffee table. She was sitting cross-legged in old jeans and a peasant blouse, stringing a hundred and eight rose quartz beads together to make prayer malas. She makes them to give away as gifts at the ashram. My parents went every year, and they were leaving tomorrow morning before dawn. "What's wrong? Is Solange all right?"

"She's fine." Mostly.

"Tell her we've asked the swami to pray for her. Why do you look so grumpy?"

"It's Nicholas. He just makes me so mad sometimes."

"Honey, you know anger poisons your body. You've always been too quick to get mad. Why do you think you have allergies? Your body's always on hyper defense."

"*Mom.*"

"Okay, okay," she said. Dad winked at me and passed the popcorn. "Are you going to be all right here on your own while we're away? I stocked the fridge."

"With tofu?" I grimaced.

"I don't want you gorging on junk food while we're away, young lady."

I rolled my eyes. "Well, I'm not eating weird tofu casseroles for two weeks." My parents had passed on their sense of social justice, even if they chose to fight with sit-ins and I preferred to swing a punch. Call it family rebellion. I felt the same way about tofu as I did about sit-ins. I'm sure they're both good for the soul, but I'd once breathed in a lungful of tear gas when my parents took me to a global warming protest and I swore I'd never lay limp in the road again. One time, Dad was hit by a rubber bullet, and the bruises on his chest had scared me more than any polluting global corporation or vicious dictator could have. Even scarier was the fact that he hadn't gotten angry, had actually lain down for it. When I turned fifteen, I was finally able to convince them to leave me behind when they went on their annual retreat.

"Maybe we should call your aunt to come stay with you," Mom said.

Not that they didn't worry.

"I was fine last year and I'll be fine this year, Mom. Besides, Lucinda's in Vegas with her new girlfriend, remember?" I crunched some popcorn. "Stop fretting, it's bad for your chi."

"She's got you there." Dad grinned.

"I'll probably stay at the Drakes' most nights anyway, just like last year," I assured her. "So, can we just watch the movie now?" I turned up the volume before she could find something else to worry about.

When the movie was over, my parents went to bed and I went back to Solange's. I'd only had my license for a few months, but the car already practically drove itself there. Although I didn't see a single person, I knew I was spotted by various guards and family members before I'd even made it onto the outskirts of the Drake compound. I didn't know why Mom was so worried; she'd already asked Bruno, the Drakes' head bodyguard, to check up on me.

The dogs didn't bother to bark when I got out. There were three of them, big, shaggy gray-black Bouviers, which looked more like bears than dogs. They might have been intimidating if they weren't currently shoving their damp noses in my pockets and whimpering for treats. I had more to fear from the windstorm they might cause with the ferocious wagging of their stubby tails.

The lamps were lit—soft yellow light gleamed through the windows. The light was always soft in the Drake house. I went around to the side, hoping Solange's bedroom window was open. I could have knocked. I usually did. It wasn't as if anyone would be asleep, and they could usually smell my presence anyway. But I didn't know if I was in trouble. I'd apologize if I was, but I hated going in unprepared. Regular parents were bad enough, but vampire parents were in a class all their own. Solange's window was closed, so I texted her. Nothing.

"Lucky."

I yelped like a scalded cat, whirling so fast I made myself dizzy. My phone landed in the bushes. Nicholas smirked at me, easing languidly out of the shadows. His pale eyes gleamed. I gasped for breath, thumping my chest. That was the second time in one night I'd practically choked on my own heart. Nicholas licked his lips. I remembered Solange's warning and tried to calm my pulse.

"What the hell, Nicky!" I muttered. He hated being called that as much as I hated being called Lucky. He stepped closer, totally invading my personal space. I hated that he was so handsome, with his tousled dark hair and his serious expression, like some ancient scholar. There was something else in his expression suddenly, something slightly wicked. I took a step back, wondering why my stomach felt funny. He advanced and I backed away some more, suspicious, until I bumped into the log wall of the house.

I remembered, too late, Solange's simplest warning about vampires: if you ran, they chased. It was just in their nature.

I stopped abruptly and lifted my chin, trying to pretend my shoulder blades weren't pressing into the log wall and I had nowhere to go.

"What?"

He was close enough that his legs practically brushed mine.

He was close enough, in point of fact, to kiss.

I was instantly horrified the thought had even crossed my mind. I tried to comfort myself with the idea that it was probably just those legendary pheromones. I was used to them, but I wasn't completely immune. And the fact was, he was looking at me the way I looked at chocolate fudge.

I bit my lower lip. He blinked, and then his face went impassive again, nearly cold; but I noticed the flare of heat in his eerie eyes.

"That was a stupid thing you did," he said.

And there was the Nicholas I knew. Of course he hadn't been flirting with me. What had I been thinking?

"It was just a party."

"It was reckless." He jerked a hand through his hair, messing it further. "We're trying to protect her. You're not making it any easier."

"You're smothering her." I scowled. "And I was protecting her, too."

"By putting her in needless danger just to flirt with some drunk kid? This isn't a game."

"I know that," I snapped. "But you don't know her like I do. And she's been so stressed out by you and your overbearing baboon brothers, I just wanted to cheer her up."

He paused, and when he spoke again it was quietly. "She can't protect herself if she's worried about protecting you."

Ouch. Direct hit. The indignation whooshed out of me, leaving me feeling deflated and foolish.

"Oh." I really hated it when he was right. "All right. Fine."

I was spared his self-satisfied reply when his cell phone rang discreetly from inside the pocket of his black cargo pants. He barely glanced at me.

"Go home. Now."

He walked away, leaving me staring at his back. I retrieved my phone to text Solange: *I do not like your brother.* I stomped all the way back to the car. The dogs had abandoned me to follow Nicholas, growling low in their throats. I kind of hoped they'd bite him. Right on the ass.

Just as I was reaching for the car door handle, a hand clamped over my shoulder and spun me around. Before I could make a single sound, Nicholas's mouth covered mine completely. He yanked me closer. His eyes were the misty gray of rain. His lips moved, briefly. It wasn't even a whisper but even that sound was hidden under the almost-but-not-quite kiss.

"We're not alone."

I stiffened.

"Shhh." He bent his head. Anyone watching would have assumed he was kissing me and enjoying it. I admit, I was enjoying it too.

A shadow moved near the hedges, too quickly to be natural. The crickets went silent. Knowing the sharpness of vampire hearing, I darted a glance pointedly over Nicholas's left shoulder. He didn't speak, didn't even nod, but I knew he understood. He kept kissing me, his tongue darting out to touch mine. It was totally distracting. He was edging me away from the car, guiding me backward, toward the house.

"Don't run." He nipped my lower lip.

"I know." Afraid I was the only one experiencing all these interesting feelings, I nipped back. His hands tightened. His mouth was on my ear when we reached the porch. By the lower step his palms moved over my waist, my hips. His lips were clever, wicked.

Perfect.

At the front door he stopped and shoved me abruptly into the foyer. I stumbled, knocking over a vase of roses. Glass shards, red petals, and water scattered over the stone floor. My lips felt swollen, tingly. *Focus, Lucy.* The hallway was already full of grim-mouthed Drake boys before I'd even caught my breath. Solange's mom pushed past me, leading them out. Nicholas was a blur between the oak trees. There were the unmistakable sounds of fighting: grunts, hissing, bones snapping.

"Are you okay?" Solange practically leaped on me.

"I'm fine."

She was heading out after her brothers when her father's voice cut through the foyer.

"Solange."

She stopped, looked over her shoulder. "They might need help."

"No."

"Dad."

"No. They're here for you. If you go out there, it will only make things worse."

I knew that look on her face. She was biting her tongue. I knew how much she hated this. Helena was the warrior in the family, had been even when she was winning martial arts competitions as a human, and she'd trained her children well. Even I'd gotten the benefit of a few tricks, but none of it would do us any good tonight. Still, I was really glad I knew how to break someone's kneecap and three ways to incapacitate using only my thumb. And to think I used to worry about midterms.

The foyer was warm and civilized, lit by warmly glowing Tiffany lamps. Liam stood between us and the battle raging in the bedraggled garden. He was nearly tall enough to obscure our vision, but we leaned sideways around him. Part of me didn't want to see what was happening; the rest of me absolutely couldn't handle not knowing. The shadows coalesced, and I watched fangs gleam and bodies jump higher than they should have been able to. The snarls lifted the hair on the back of my neck.

Nicholas was fast and clever but I'd never seen him like this before. His face was hard as he leaped and dodged, sent his boot into the midsection of a vampire not much older than us, with long blond hair. They both tumbled, but only Nicholas landed on his feet. I felt inordinately proud about that.

All of Solange's brothers held their own, but only Quinn appeared to be enjoying himself. He grinned even as a fist, moving so fast it was a flesh-colored blur, broke his nose. Blood trickled down to his lip and he licked it. Helena laughed behind him, somersaulting out of the way of a stake and landing behind her attacker. He disintegrated in a cloud of dust at her feet.

"I want one alive and able to speak," Liam called out. He shook his head at Solange. "Honestly, your mother's worse than the boys. Helena"—he raised his voice slightly—"leave me one, damn it."

"Spoilsport," she muttered before reining herself in. Her flying kick only knocked the vampire into a tree instead of shattering his ribs. Hyacinth made a small sound behind us. The jet beads around her neck caught the light, glimmered.

"That's hardly ladylike," she said disapprovingly. Which was amusing since I'd heard the stories of what she did in her spare time—and it wasn't taking tea and eating cucumber sandwiches.

A vampire fled, disappearing into the woods. One of them shuddered, turned to ash, and drifted into the hedges. The stake tumbled to the ground. Solange's second-oldest brother, Sebastian, wiped his hands off dispassionately and then turned to help his mother drag the half-conscious vampire she'd thrown into the tree toward the house. Connor was speaking quietly into his cell phone to Bruno.

I pressed my back against the wall as a parade of teeth and feral smiles passed me. When they were all gathered in the parlor, I followed. I went to my favorite purple velvet armchair by the fireplace. Solange stood next to me, her eyes never leaving that of the young man currently being tied up. His shirt was torn, his dark reddish brown hair pulled back into a ponytail. His eyelids fluttered but didn't open. I wouldn't have opened them either if all seven Drake brothers were standing around me, glaring. Never mind Helena, who waved them aside with barely a flick of her wrist. She sniffed once, delicately.

"He smells like kith." She whispered but shook her head. "Kind of."

Liam frowned, sniffed as well.

"Something's not right." His gaze narrowed, sharpened. "Left arm."

We all looked even though I didn't know what I was looking at. The tip of a tattoo poked out from under his pushed-up sleeve. It looked like a stylized tribal-style sun but I couldn't be sure.

"Damn," Nicholas muttered. "Helios-Ra."

Everyone looked totally bummed out over such a comic-book name. He stirred. There was a gentle waft of lilies and chocolate, almost right, but not quite. Everyone else was still scenting the air like hunting hounds, nostrils flared.

"What?" I whispered to Solange. "What's with all the sniffing? It's creeping me out."

She didn't have time to answer because he opened his eyes, suddenly, as if he'd been poked with something sharp. His eyes weren't pale, not like every other vampire's I'd ever seen.

They were very black and very hostile.

CHAPTER 3

◆

Solange

"You're . . . m-mortal," I finally stammered. I knew Lucy liked to think all vampires had this suave quality, but I so didn't, and not just because I wasn't technically a vampire yet. She was the one with the beaded velvet scarves, and I was the one with the pottery clay dried on my pants. Plus, I was totally gaping at him. He was a hunter, and he worked for an organization devoted to wiping us out. The sun tattoo was proof enough of that, underscored by his expression: righteous anger.

Great.

"I don't get it," Lucy whispered to me. "Who is he?"

"Not one of us," I whispered back, my gaze never leaving his. I didn't know what I was reading there, but it was complicated, whatever it was. I'd heard of the cologne some hunters wore; it mimicked vampire pheromones, to take a potential enemy off guard. We'd believed it completely out in the garden, until he'd had to fight my mother, who would have killed him if my dad hadn't been so adamant about having someone to question.

Nicholas half stepped in front of us, annoyingly overprotective as always. He didn't like surprises and unanswered questions and we'd just had our fill of both. I'd been trained just like they had, but none of my brothers could get it in their thick heads that I wasn't delicate or defenseless.

The Helios-Ra agent was wearing black nose plugs, which just proved he knew more about us than we knew about him. I reached over and yanked them out.

"What are you doing here?" I could tell he was trying to hold his breath. I could've told him that strategy never worked for long. He glared at me mutinously.

"Tracking," he finally answered on a sharp exhale.

"Let me guess," I said, disgusted. "Because I'm just so beautiful and you don't know why but you just have to be with me?" I was really starting to hate this whole pheromone thing.

He blinked, nearly smiled. "Not exactly."

I blinked back. "Oh." Damn it, he was even more attractive when he didn't seem particularly affected by my questionable charms. "Well, who are you then?"

"Helios-Ra," he answered, his tone clipped.

"Yeah, we got that."

"Your name?" Dad scowled.

"Kieran Black."

"Since when has Helios-Ra been on our trail? Last time I checked, we had a treaty. We don't eat humans, so you don't bother us and we don't bother you."

My mom snorted. She hated the treaty. She preferred fighting, being much more skilled with weapons than tact, but my dad was all about practicality and the long view. He'd made the treaty before my oldest brother was born, determined to give his children a chance. He didn't want us being harassed and followed about by the league just because we're vampires. After all, vampires aren't all good or all bad, any more than humans are. But try telling that to the Helios-Ra. They only recently admitted that being a vampire wasn't a good enough reason to be killed on sight. Still, old traditions die hard with them, almost as hard as with us.

But our family, at least, has a good reputation. We mostly drink animal blood, only resorting to human blood if it's consensual or if we're ill and can't heal without it. If that fails, a quick break-in at the blood bank works well enough. We've never gone feral; the disease has been in our bloodline too many centuries for that, and every generation is born stronger than the last. It's not easy dying, even if you know you're going to wake up afterward. And it's even harder controlling the bloodthirst. Still, hardly any of us go mad anymore during the turning. I had to remind myself of that little fact every time I looked at the calendar to see my birthday edging closer and closer. Lucy nudged me.

"You're looking morose," she said under her breath. "You're thinking about it again."

I turned my attention back to the matter at hand. I couldn't afford to get sidetracked with self-pity—or by the fact that this particular Helios-Ra agent was really good-looking, with his dark eyes and strong cheekbones.

"Things change," he said. "You should know. You broke the treaty."

Mom's eyes narrowed dangerously.

"I beg your pardon?" she said, soft as a mouse near a sleeping cat.

Uh-oh. Mom was big on that whole honor thing.

"Big mistake," Lucy said pleasantly. She was a lot more blood-thirsty than I was, ironically enough. She would have made a better vampire than me. I shot her a look.

"What?" she asked innocently. "He was after you, he deserves it."

Nicholas barely turned his head. "Do you two mind?"

"Yeah, yeah," she muttered.

Mom stepped up close enough that Kieran was sweating a little and breathing as shallowly as he could. Our pheromones when we were distracting mortals to drink was nothing compared with the pheromones when we were angry. His entire body was probably flooding with adrenaline, trying to decide between fight or flight. I couldn't sense it yet, but soon enough I'd be able to taste it on my tongue like champagne bubbles. It wasn't a particularly comforting thought.

"Are you accusing us of breaking an oath?" Mom's voice was like broken glass—glittery and dangerous. Beside her, Sebastian bared his teeth. His fangs were retracted, but still, there was something too sharp about his teeth. He barely spoke, even to us, and his silence was terrifying to those who didn't know him.

"It's common knowledge."

"Is it?"

"Drakes," he spat. "I know better than to trust any of you."

Byron, one of the dogs, growled. Quinn smiled.

"Let me talk to him," he suggested. There was always something slightly violent about his smiles. Dad held up his hand. Quinn subsided, but barely.

"We haven't broken the treaty," Dad said quietly.

"Helios-Ra says you have."

"Then Helios-Ra is misinformed. And I won't have your organization endangering my daughter."

He glanced at me, glanced away.

"If you keep me here, you really will be breaking the treaty." He was breathing through his mouth, as if that would help.

"Actually, since you broke the treaty by coming here in the first place"—Dad's voice was silky—"we really needn't concern ourselves with those rules." Mom actually smirked.

"I . . ."

"How old are you?" Dad asked.

"Eighteen."

Dad shook his head, dismayed. "They're training them younger and younger."

"They need to be able to infiltrate the high schools and colleges to spy on us," Connor pointed out.

"I'm only doing my job. Keeping people safe from monsters like you."

"People like you are the reason my aunt Ruby won't leave her house anymore," I snapped. She'd lost her husband and three sons to hunters and had never really recovered from the loss.

His face went hard. "Monsters like you are the reason my father's dead."

"Oh and we've never lost family members to hunters or Helios?" I shot back even though I felt bad that he'd lost his father.

"And they're not monsters, you bigot," Lucy broke in, incensed. She leaped to her feet. "It's a disease, you ignorant prig. Are people with diabetes or arthritis monsters too?" If secrecy wasn't so important, she would have used her theory in her personal crusade to make the world accept us.

"It's not the same."

"It is *so.*"

"My dad's throat was ripped out."

There was silence. Then Dad frowned. "Only the *Hel-Blar* rip out throats, son."

"A vampire's a vampire," Kieran insisted stubbornly. Lucy went red in the face.

"Why are you really here?" Dad pressed before she could explode.

"Because of the bounty," he answered tightly.

Mom went unnaturally still. Her eyes caught the light and reflected it. "What bounty?"

"The bounty on the Drake family."

Someone snarled. The air was so charged I was vaguely surprised it didn't spark and catch fire. Dad stalked toward the phone on the desk. He barked orders into the receiver, not even bothering with a greeting. "Double the patrols. Get word to everyone. Yes, even her. And the council." He switched to the cell phone in his pocket, dialing grimly. His voice muted to a soft murmur I couldn't entirely make out. My hearing wasn't sharp enough. Yet.

"What the hell's the bounty for?" Sebastian demanded.

"I don't know."

Quinn sauntered over, leaned in close. "You'll tell us."

Kieran paled slightly, trying to break eye contact. Quinn's hand closed over his throat. Kieran seemed a little dazed when he finally answered.

"It was posted tonight." He shuddered. Sweat beaded on his upper lip.

"Is this about Solange?"

"I don't know." He choked, tried to swallow. "I don't know," he repeated. "I heard there was a bounty, and I wanted in." Something in his voice made me think it was less about the bounty and more about the chance to stick it to our family specifically.

Quinn eased back, letting his hand drop to his side. "Some agency, attacking a fifteen-year-old girl." He spat. "Cowards."

Kieran took several deep ragged breaths. "We protect the innocent."

"This isn't a comic book, idiot," Lucy muttered crossly.

"If you're going to kill me too, get it over with."

"We don't drink from people like you," Nicholas sneered, making it sound as insulting as he could.

"Do you drink from her?" Kieran nodded at Lucy. "Have you made her your slave?"

"Who, Lucy?" Nicholas snickered.

"Hey!" Lucy snapped. "Shut up."

I wasn't entirely sure which one she was talking to.

"This isn't getting us anywhere," Duncan said quietly. Like Sebastian, he rarely lost his temper or his focus. "Let's not get sidetracked." He tied a black bandana over Kieran's mouth, knotting it securely. Dad nodded approvingly before pointing toward the kitchen.

"Kitchen. Now."

◆

Our kitchen looked like any farm kitchen: a huge wooden table, ladderback chairs, painted cupboards, and a kettle on the stove. There was a basket on the counter full of red apples and pomegranates and even food in the fridge, mostly for me and for Lucy when she stayed over. In fact, she was already pouring herself a glass of cranberry juice. The blood was kept in an old wine cellar, hidden in the wall and locked with three deadbolts and an alarm system. That was a fairly new precaution, ever since one of Logan's ex-girlfriend's brothers had barged in after Logan had broken up with his sister. The guards hadn't stopped him; it would have seemed suspicious to have them swarm out just because someone came to the front door uninvited. The dogs had stopped him though, even before Mom had. He hadn't made it past the front hall. It was only luck that he hadn't seen into the kitchen, with the jug of blood on the counter. Needless to say, we were strongly encouraged not to date humans after that.

Now Quinn paced beside that same counter; Nicholas leaned against the wall, arms crossed. The rest of my brothers sat, though their muscles were tensed for sudden movement. I watched the dark fields on the other side of the glass with suspicion. Dad's phone rang again. Mom glanced at Lucy.

"We should call your parents."

"Can't." She set her glass down. "They're at the ashram for two weeks, remember?" The sun was edging up over the horizon. "And they always leave early to watch the sun rise over the lake."

She sighed. "Of course. You'll stay here then."

"I will? But no one's after me."

"You're part of this family, young lady, and your mother would never forgive me if I left you unprotected, especially now," Mom told Lucy sternly.

"Yes, ma'am." My mother was the only person on the planet who was able to get that meek tone out of Lucy. No one else would have even known it existed. I dropped into the chair next to her and stole a sip of her juice. I tried not to imagine what it would be like to drink blood instead. My stomach tilted.

"This is unacceptable," Aunt Hyacinth fumed. "The Drake family has a good and honorable name. They've no right to do this. We're on the council."

"Let's go straight to the Helios-Ra headquarters," Quinn added, his expression hard. "I can clear this up."

"As if your temper has ever helped us." Logan snorted.

"Careful, little brother."

They were all talking over each other until my mother cleared her throat.

"Boys."

Silence fell, reluctantly but quickly. Dad switched off his

phone. There were lines around his mouth I'd never seen before. "The boy was right. Bounty's been set."

Mom cursed. "Why?" she asked.

"That may take a while to figure out. There've been a few disappearances, rumors that don't make sense. I've got people on it." He leaned down on the counter, his fists clenched. "I've put a call in to Hart and to Lady Natasha."

"Natasha?" Aunt Hyacinth frowned. "Is that wise? She exiled us all."

"I know." Hart was the head of the Helios-Ra and not a fan of Lady Natasha. "Until we know more, no one leaves this property alone. Solange, you don't leave at all."

"Why am I the only one under house arrest? That's so unfair."

"Solange, you know why."

"I know how to take care of myself." I gritted my teeth.

"Yes, you do. But you know as well as I do that you're not at your full strength."

"But I feel *fine*." I was so tired of saying it over and over again. I already felt trapped, smothered. I'd chew off my own foot like an animal caught in a leg trap if they didn't give me some space.

"Sol," Nicholas said softly. "Please."

I hissed out a frustrated breath. When I looked at my mom, I made sure my chin was up, my gaze steady. "I still get to go to my shed." If they tried to keep me from the kiln and my pottery wheel, I'd be insane by my birthday. Mom must have seen my desperation.

"Agreed."

I let out another breath. "Okay."

Dad's phone rang again. He listened quietly before motioning to Sebastian and Connor. "Your uncle Geoffrey is on his way. And your aunt Ruby's arriving; go on and help her inside." The fact that Ruby had been persuaded to leave her house for ours spoke volumes as to the seriousness of the situation. Dad touched Mom's hand, his mouth tight. "We'll figure this out," he promised before sending us all up to our respective bedrooms.

"Are you okay?" Lucy asked me as we got ready for bed. She started by taking off the pounds of silver jewelry she always wore—proving that it's only a myth that vampires can't tolerate silver.

"I'm fine, it's everyone else who's losing it," I muttered.

She snorted. "Big surprise. You're the baby sister and you *know* how your brothers get."

I rolled my eyes. "What's it like being an only child?"

"How would I know? Your brothers harass me just as much as they harass you."

"True."

Lucy waited until we'd changed into our pajamas before speaking again. She wore a long black cotton nightgown that looked like a sundress, and I wore my favorite flannel pj bottoms and a T-shirt. Out of the two of us, she always looked like the one who should be turning into a vampire. I sighed.

"Sol," she said. "I never saw Nicholas's bloodchange, or Logan's. I was banned from the house, remember?"

"I remember," I said softly. I hadn't been kicked out of the house, but I certainly hadn't been welcomed on the third floor, where all my brothers slept. I'd heard the unnatural silence and seen my parents' pale, worried faces as they took shifts sitting with Logan and then Nicholas the next year. With my other brothers I'd been too young to really know what was happening, and my parents had sent me off for slumber parties at Lucy's. Her mother had fussed over me and fed me chocolate, which made Lucy cranky since she only ever got to eat carob. I hadn't really understood it then.

I understood it now.

"So . . . what really happens?" Lucy pressed. "I know you get sick, but is it as bad as all that?"

It really was.

"No, it's fine," I lied as we climbed into our respective beds. "I mean, it's not fun or anything, but you know the Drakes. We love a good overprotective melodrama."

Yup, totally lying.

And I could tell Lucy wasn't really buying it. She opened her mouth to ask me another question. A soft knock at the door interrupted her. She shot me a glare like I'd orchestrated it.

"Sol, it's me," Nicholas murmured from the other side of the door. "Can I come in?"

"Sure," I said as Lucy sat up suddenly and smoothed her hair. I blinked at her. Since when did she care what she looked like for any of my brothers? The door didn't make a sound on its hinges as Nicholas slipped inside. He was wearing his black pants but no shirt, like he'd been interrupted changing. Clearly something was up. Just as clearly, Lucy was trying not to stare at his chest. He flicked her a glance, frowned.

"What?"

She jerked her eyes away. "Nothing." She looked like she might be blushing. I was definitely going to bug her about that later. For now, it would have to wait.

"What's up?" I asked him.

"Someone's downstairs," he said quietly. "He scratched at the window and Dad let him in after Mom threatened to eat his face."

"Ew," Lucy said.

"Vampire."

"Lurking at the windows?" I slid out from under my blanket. "That's not good."

"They're in the library."

We looked at each other, then nodded and hurried out to the hall without another word. The library was one of the only rooms in the house where we could properly eavesdrop. We'd discovered, thanks to a tip from Quinn, that if you lie on the floor in the spare guest room next to mine and pressed your ear to the vent, you could pretty much hear everything that was going on.

We stretched out on the hardwood and wriggled into position. Nicholas was between us, hogging the best listening spot. His face was turned toward Lucy.

"I can't hear—" He pressed his finger to her lips to stop her from saying anything else. My parents would hear us if we whispered right over the vent. There were definite disadvantages to having vampire parents: sneaking around was nearly impossible. At least come my birthday, I wouldn't be the only one clomping around the house deaf to all the intrigue. I'd hear as well as them.

"Is there a single reason why we shouldn't stake you where you stand?" my mom asked pleasantly.

"I'm not here for the bounty," a male voice assured her. It was low and rumbly, as if it came from a really big chest. I couldn't help but imagine a wrestler down in the library. "I would hardly announce my presence, would I?"

"You didn't exactly knock at the front door," Dad said drily.

"There are humans in this house," he said as if that was explanation enough. "I smell at least two, but not here in this room." If we were really lucky, he wouldn't smell Lucy and me over his head before we heard what else he had to say.

"I've come to offer my allegiance to your daughter."

On second thought, I could have done without hearing that.

"Have you?" Mom didn't sound convinced. Dad was probably overjoyed at the thought of negotiating another alliance. I kind of just wanted to go back to bed.

"You're sworn to Lady Natasha," Dad said softly. "You wear the mark of her house."

"I'm sworn to the royal court, yes." It was an important distinction. "But there are those of us who would rather oath to the House of Drake, and I am here representing them."

Crap. That prophecy thing again. Why didn't anyone believe me when I said I didn't want to be a princess or a queen or whatever? I didn't want to be the excuse for a civil war within the tribes. I shuddered.

"We'll keep that in mind. We'd need proof of your loyalty, of course."

"Of course. When the time comes, you'll get your proof." He sounded like he was bowing. "Until then."

I heard the window shut and Mom and Dad moved out of the

library. I sighed and closed my eyes. I'd felt fine all day but now I was exhausted, almost like I had the flu.

"I'm sorry I almost left you behind," Nicholas whispered tightly to Lucy. "I really thought they'd follow us and you'd be safer at the party.

What?" he asked when she didn't immediately respond.

"You've never apologized to me before."

"I said I was sorry the time I used your doll for target practice with the pellet gun."

"Because your mom had you by the ear."

"Well, whatever. Sorry."

"Thanks," she whispered.

"You're welcome," he whispered back.

I suddenly felt like a third wheel. Weird.

Nicholas scrambled to his feet. "We should go."

"She's asleep," Lucy said. I wasn't, but I didn't have the energy to tell her that.

"I've got her," Nicholas said grimly, picking me up and carrying me to my room.

CHAPTER 4

◆

Lucy

Saturday morning

Mornings were always quiet in the Drake household, even with nearly twenty people stuffed into its tiny rooms and narrow halls. Sunlight sparkled at the windows, made of some sort of treated glass. Ancient vampires can stand sunlight though they never really love it, but it dangerously weakens the younger ones, who haven't had a chance to build up an immunity. I never took sunlight for granted now, or my ability to eat every meal with cutlery. Though, aside from the whole blood thing, the Drakes were very civilized. They used glasses and goblets, not plastic blood bags.

Lady Natasha, by all accounts, was *not* civilized. She'd been Montmartre's second-in-command and his lover. When he'd tired of her, she allied herself with a powerful vampire family. She knew the customs of the vampires, the Host, and the Hounds, and she was determined to bring them all together under her leadership. Biases ran deeply though, and so far she hadn't managed to unite them. It wasn't for an altruistic motive like ending what was basically a civil war; it was all about the power for her. And possibly sticking it to Montmartre.

I'd seen the roses with his name on them.

They didn't bode well. He clearly wanted a Drake daughter to give him vampire babies—and the power of the council and the royal courts if Solange really did take them over. He wanted it all.

Lady Natasha, who wanted him as much as she wanted power, wouldn't be too keen on any part of that plan.

If only vampire politics were on high school history exams, I'd be all set.

Solange was still asleep, curled around the sunbeams falling on her pillow. I'd already noticed that she was sleeping later and later. I was starting to get nervous for her. Everyone else seemed to think it was a totally normal part of the change. I pulled a sweater on over my nightgown and added thick socks. It was always freezing in the Drake house, no matter the time of year. I went straight to the kitchen to make myself some tea and toast. No one else was awake. I ate my breakfast and then took my tea with me as I wandered through the house.

In my sleep-dazed state, I'd actually forgotten about Kieran, tied to a sturdy chair in one of the parlors. I froze, cup halfway to my mouth. His eyes were intent, curious, edgy. I might not like his attitude, but I guessed I'd be edgy too if I was tied up in a vampire's house. Especially if I was a brainwashed Helios-Ra agent.

The gag was loose around his neck, lying next to his nose plugs. In daylight I noticed he was wearing black jeans and a black shirt, with bare straps where Helena had removed his weapons.

"You look like you belong in a bad comic book," I told him cheerfully.

He stared at me. "You really aren't bothered by the whole vampire thing, are you?"

I shrugged. "Whatever." It was obvious he didn't know what to make of me. I approached curiously. I'd never actually seen a Helios-Ra agent before. I wondered what the fuss was about. He was barely older than we were. His hands were lashed loosely at the wrists so he could move them a little, but his shoulders were tied tighter to the chair back. He wore steel-toed army boots, also attached tightly at the ankles. "What did the Drakes do that's got you all pissy?"

"Pissy? Did you just call me pissy?"

"I call 'em how I see 'em."

"You are the weirdest girl."

"From the guy who thinks he's a secret agent man."

"You should take the Helios-Ra more seriously," he warned me.

I smiled at him with very little humor. "I don't take direction well." I raised my eyebrows. "So? What's with the vendetta?"

His jaw clenched. "I told you."

"I'm sorry your dad died. But you can't blame all vampires for the actions of one." I tried to sound reasonable, calming. My mom was a natural at that sort of thing. Me? Not so much. "That's called racism."

"They're not human."

"That's so beside the point."

He gaped at me. "What?"

"And besides, the Drakes are human, or were mostly. And they've never gone all rogue and fangy on the general populace. Don't they teach you anything at that hotshot secret academy?"

"How did you know about the academy?" He was trying not to look startled.

"Please. It's kind of obvious."

"You don't understand."

"I understand exactly," I said.

"They've brainwashed you."

"Hey, you're the one in some kind of hunter cult."

He narrowed his eyes. "This isn't a joke, Lucy. The Drakes killed my father."

"They did *not*."

"You don't even know who my father is."

"I know you're an idiot."

He looked at me for a long silent moment as if he was searching for something. Then he looked at my cup.

"Can I have a sip?" he asked. "I haven't had anything to drink all night."

I didn't trust him, obviously. He'd scaled several fences and snuck onto a heavily guarded vampire land with less than polite intentions. Still, it was only tea. How dangerous could that be? I stepped closer. I lifted the cup to his lips and he drank gratefully.

"I'm sorry," he whispered, smiling sadly. He slipped his right hand under his left cuff and there was a small cracking sound and a puff that looked like powdered sugar from a vial sewn into his sleeve. The heavy scents of chocolate and lilies hung between us. It made me want to sneeze.

"I'm pretty much immune to vampire pheromones," I informed him loftily, crossing my arms.

He didn't look disappointed or defeated.

"You're not immune to this blend," he said.

"Yes, I am. I don't know what you think—" The room wavered slightly, like I was seeing it through heat waves coming off asphalt. "What the hell?"

Another puff of powder.

"This is a special blend." He sounded briefly apologetic. "No one can resist it for long."

"You're not going to get away with this." All the colors looked weird, as if they were full of light. The red of the velvet drapes looked as if it were dripping blood. "I'll scream." I opened my mouth.

"You will not scream," he said calmly.

I closed my mouth. The taste of cocoa and flowers made me gag. There was something else laced under the flavors, but I couldn't place it. Licorice, whiskey, something. I felt faint, befuddled. And underneath the vagueness, fiery anger.

"Untie me, Lucy."

My hands fluttered forward.

"No," I whispered, watching them as if they belonged to somebody else. I curled my fingers into my palms. Sweat beaded under my hair, on my face. My glasses slipped down my nose. "No."

"Untie me, Lucy," he demanded, more forcefully. "I'm

impressed. Few people need a repetition. But you can't win against it—you'll only hurt yourself trying."

I fought the compulsion frantically, and lost. The knots loosened, fell free. When his hands were unbound, he wiggled out of the shoulder ropes and then bent down to untie his ankles.

"Stay there, Lucy. Don't make a sound, don't make a move until I'm gone."

I struggled and strained but it was like sticky chains held me tight. The Drakes were going to kill me. I had freed their only advantage, who was now lifting the window open and slipping out into the ragged garden. At least he didn't know about the silent alarms. Still, they weren't enough. I watched him hop the decorative stone wall, run across the field, and slip into the forest. The sun beamed brightly on his head. I heard footsteps, a soft curse, and Nicholas's furious voice.

"What the hell have you done?"

The release was abrupt and total. My muscles felt like water. My vision grayed and I crumpled to the carpet. I didn't pass out but it took me a moment to open my eyes again, a longer moment for all the furniture to settle back down into their proper places. Nicholas was crouched beside me, eyes gleaming.

"You little idiot."

The last of the spiderweb-sticky film of compulsion dissolved. I was eager to reestablish myself, panic running like angry ferrets through me at the thought that the effects might be permanent. The anxiety had me nauseous. I reared up suddenly, as if I'd been poked with a cattle prod. The exhilaration of controlling my limbs again was sweeter than any chocolate.

Nicholas, possibly, didn't agree.

"You have *got* to stop breaking my nose!" he hollered as the rest of the family thundered in. Blood stained his fingers as he cracked his nose back into place.

"Oops," I said, wincing. It was probably a good thing he healed so quickly. I rubbed my forehead where I'd crashed into his nose. My breathing was uneven, as if I'd been underwater too long. Quinn, only half-dressed, glared at the chair with the empty ropes coiled like sleeping snakes. His expression went hot, then cold.

"Where the hell is he?"

"She let him go," Nicholas explained tightly, rising from his crouch. It was then I finally noticed he was wearing only pj bottoms. His chest was bare, roped with slender muscles. My breathing sounded loud, even to me. The combined weight of the Drakes' outraged fury made me cringe. More adrenaline pumped into my bloodstream. Great. I already felt as if I'd drunk a gallon of espresso. I didn't know if I was going to pass out or explode. Solange helped steady me.

"Are you okay?"

"I think so." My teeth were chattering. I fought back tears of frustration and guilt burning behind my eyelids. Nicholas heaved a disgusted sigh before wrapping me roughly in an afghan and shoving me onto the couch.

"You're practically green," he muttered, pushing my head down between my knees. "Breathe."

Helena was at the window, snarling. She shaded her eyes. The glass might make the sunlight safe but their eyes were still pale and sensitive.

"I'm sorry," I said miserably. "I only meant to give him a sip of tea. He said he was thirsty." I could tell Liam was reining in his temper with a formidable amount of willpower. The tendons on his neck stood out in stark relief. His jaw might have been carved out of marble.

"What happened?" he asked very slowly, very precisely.

I wanted to crawl into a hole.

"He blew some sort of powder in my face." I rubbed my chilled arms. I wondered if it was a side effect of the drug or if I was in shock. "I resisted it at first, it was kind of like your pheromones. But the second dose did me in. He told me to untie him." I closed my eyes briefly, irritated with myself. "And I did. I couldn't stop myself."

"Willingly?" Quinn hollered. "On purpose?"

Liam silenced him with a look and came to sit in front of me. I tried to avoid his eyes, gave up. There was mostly hard patience and very little recrimination in his face.

"I'm so sorry. I tried to fight it. It was like being hypnotized or something."

"I need you to tell me everything you remember."

I described the way it tasted, that it tickled my nose, clung to my sweater.

"Hypnos," Liam said coldly. Helene turned from her post. She pointed to the desk, and Connor went to retrieve a little jeweled box from the bottom drawer. Then he used a small brush to collect whatever powdery residue he could from my sweater and the carpet.

"We've never been able to get our hands on any," Liam explained smugly. "We'll have Geoffrey analyze it." Geoffrey taught night classes in biology at the local college. But he also had his own lab and was always running experiments and studying the Drakes' unique gifts.

"But what is it?"

"We're not sure about all the components; certainly it contains one of the zombie herbs. The rest, we don't know enough about, only that it's very powerful. Apparently, we should have searched him more thoroughly."

"It was hidden in his sleeve." I scowled. "If I ever see him again, I'm going to shove it right—"

"Stay away from him," Nicholas interrupted my rant. I ignored him.

"Now what do we do?" I asked.

"Now we go back to bed and get some rest," Liam reminded me gently. "Let us worry about it." Solange yawned wide enough to split her face. The brothers were all paler than usual, dark circles like bruises under their water-colored eyes. They were still young. In fact, Logan had only turned two years ago. He was so exhausted he looked drunk, barely able to stand up by himself. Sebastian propped him up, leading him toward the staircase. Nicholas had been turned even more recently than that, so I assumed only his irritation with me was keeping him upright.

Solange yawned again. "Are you going to be okay?"

I nodded. "Go on back to bed." It was nearly eleven but she was weaving a little on her feet. The rest of the family wandered off to their respective private quarters, Liam and Helena whispering to each other. Liam was already dialing his cell phone. Only Nicholas remained. He was the color of milk.

"Aren't you going up?" I asked.

He stepped closer to me.

"In a minute."

I finally felt warm. The afghan slipped from my shoulders. He was looking at me as if he wanted to peel me open like an orange. I remembered the feel of his mouth on mine. I frowned, nervous for no reason.

"What?"

"I just want to try something." His touch was gentle, skimming my cheek, my arm, down to my wrist. His eyes were like rain in autumn; violent, mysterious, beautiful.

Hypnotizing.

"Stop it," I whispered.

"Stay away from Kieran," he demanded softly. "He's dangerous."

"And you're not?"

"Let's find out." He closed the distance between us before I had time to even blink.

"What are you doing?"

"I have no idea," he admitted. His lips hovered just barely a breath away from mine.

"I thought you were mad at me." I really wanted to lean forward, just ever so slightly.

"I am."

"You're also trying to use your vamp mojo on me."

"It doesn't work on you."

"Remember that." My voice was soft, like whipped cream, and at odds with my smug smirk.

Lucy

We didn't close our eyes, not even when our lips met. I tingled all the way down to my toes. I wasn't remotely chilled anymore; in fact, it felt like the longest, most humid day of summer. His skin was cool. I kind of wanted to nip into him like he was ice cream. When his tongue touched mine, my eyelids finally drifted shut. I gave myself to the moment, all but hurled into it. I wanted it to last for the next year and a half at least. I'd never felt like this before.

It could totally become addictive.

Just imagine if we actually *liked* each other.

CHAPTER 5

◆

Solange

Saturday afternoon

When I woke up, Lucy was muttering to herself. It wasn't unusual, but there was a particularly strident edge to it, even more than was ordinarily the result of her impatience with our slow Internet connection. The several farms comprising the Drake compound were nearly a thousand acres, some without any power source. Our house was lucky to have satellite service even if it meant our connection suffered when it was a cloudy day somewhere else on the continent.

"Stupid satellite."

I'd need a calculator to figure out how many times I'd woken up to her yelling at my computer. Patience was not one of Lucy's finer qualities. I snuggled deeper into the nest of blankets. The sun seemed a little too bright, but I liked the warmth of it on my face. "What time is it?" I yawned.

Lucy flicked me a glance. "Just past two, I think." She scribbled on a piece of paper. "Nose plugs, definitely need those. And a pocket knife, something really pointy. Ooh!" She interrupted herself excitedly. "A stun gun. Think they sell those on eBay?"

I yawned again, pushed myself up on my elbow. I was more tired than usual but I ignored that. "What on earth are you doing now?" I asked.

"Making a list of supplies," she answered grimly. "I have no intention of letting that Helios-Ra jerkface use me to get to you again."

"It wasn't your fault."

She didn't look remotely convinced. "Nicholas thinks it's my fault."

"Since when do you care what he thinks?"

She paused. "Oh. Good point." She clicked the mouse. "Hey, look, they do have stun guns. That one has Hello Kitty on it, I think. Maybe not, it's hard to tell." Her eyes widened comically. "What are they made out of, solid gold and diamonds? I can't afford that on my allowance."

I groaned, letting my head fall back on my pillow. "Lucy, you can't order one of those. Not exactly subtle."

She made a face. "I guess."

"Besides, you know my mom's probably got one in the storeroom."

She swiveled on her chair, eyes shining. "Think she'd give me one?"

"After last time? Not a chance."

"What, come on! That was ages ago."

"No one's forgotten what happened when you convinced her to teach you archery."

"How was I supposed to know I'd have such good aim?"

She'd very nearly skewered Marcus through the heart, which would have killed him, like anyone else. Arrows worked as well as stakes; it didn't matter what the material was, as long as it was pointy and went right through the heart. It was actually fairly difficult to do: rib cages weren't easy to pierce. She frowned at me.

"You're really pale. Are you feeling okay?" she asked.

"God, not you, too." I pulled the pillow over my face. "I'm *fine*."

"You're crabby."

"Because you're bugging me."

She poked me. "I haven't even begun to bug you."

I uncovered one eye. "Go away, Luce. I'm tired." I tried to make my one exposed eye do that cold flare thing my mom was so good at. Lucy tilted her head.

"You're getting better at that."

The one thing about being best friends with someone for so long was that even turning into a vampire didn't really faze her. Her smile softened. Great. My vampire mojo engendered pity, not fear.

"Go back to sleep," she said. The light caught the sequins on her velvet scarf, making me blink. "I'll keep making lists of the painful and very slow ways I can make Kieran suffer."

Kieran.

I closed my eyes, wondering why it was no effort at all to call up the exact shade of his dark eyes, hostile as they were. I should be thinking about the bounty on our heads, not whether or not I'd get to see him again. Because of course I'd get to see him again; he'd probably try and stake one of my brothers, if not me. Hardly a promising start to a relationship.

Relationship?

What the hell was I thinking?

No doubt my impending birthday was making my head fuzzy. There was no other explanation. I just needed more sleep. Because I did feel more tired than usual, as if keeping my eyes open was becoming a ridiculously difficult task, on par with algorithms and Hyacinth's needlepoint. When I woke up again, I was alone in my room. My stomach grumbled loudly. I felt better, rested and clearly hungry. Maybe I'd make myself waffles with blueberry syrup. I couldn't imagine ever not wanting to eat my way through a huge pile of them with whipped cream, even if every single one of my brothers assured me that by this time next week the very thought would make me nauseous. So I'd better eat as much as I could, while I still could.

The house was still quiet. The sun hadn't set yet, my brothers would still be asleep. My dad could stay up all day and could even sit outside under a shady tree. But today, I knew, he'd be on the phone with every operative and vamp he knew, and Mom was probably taking inventory of the weapons. She wasn't very strong during the day yet, but she wouldn't be able to sit still—not after last night.

The kitchen was empty though Lucy had left a pot of coffee warming for me. I poured myself a cup and though it tasted good,

I wasn't in the mood for food anymore. We were out of blueberry syrup anyway. When my parents went shopping for groceries, they tended to bring home bloody steak and anything red: raspberries, cherries, hot peppers. It didn't make cooking easy.

"Darling, try the raspberry mousse. It's fresh."

Neither did Aunt Hyacinth.

I tried to conceal a shudder as I turned on one heel to smile at her. She stood in the doorway, wearing what I called her Victorian bordello dressing gown: all lace and velvet flowers and silk fringe. Her long brown hair was caught in a messy knot. Her pug, Mrs. Brown, sniffled at her feet. If Mrs. Brown was out of Aunt Hyacinth's rooms, then it followed that the other dogs, giant babies that they were, were currently cowering under the dining room table. They feared Mrs. Brown the way I feared reality TV.

"Come up for a chat," Aunt Hyacinth invited after pouring herself a glass of cherry cordial. She liked to experiment with flavoring her blood-laced food and drink.

Which is why I had absolutely no intention of touching the raspberry mousse.

We could technically eat food after the bloodchange, only it had virtually no taste and absolutely no nutritional value for us. Only blood kept us alive and healthy. Gross, gross, gross.

I was so going to have to get over this blood phobia of mine.

And soon.

"Are you coming?" Aunt Hyacinth called from the top of the staircase. I followed her up, Mrs. Brown nipping at my heels enthusiastically. There was a canine whine from the dining room.

Aunt Hyacinth had a suite of rooms on the second floor, as did my parents and I, next to one of the guest rooms. Aunt Hyacinth preferred to live with us instead of building her own house on the Drake compound. She could certainly afford it. Our family had been around long enough to learn how to be comfortably wealthy. At first there was considerable theft involved, which no one ever reported, thanks to the pheromones. But in the last few hundred years, everyone had begun stockpiling coins and decorative pieces, which turned into very valuable antiques with very little effort. In fact, every child born or made in the Drake family had a trust fund begun in their name in the form of a chest full of antique gold locked in the basement safe room. But, wealth notwithstanding, Aunt Hyacinth claimed being alone too much made her maudlin. Her word, not mine; though according to Lucy's school friends I had a weird vocabulary and a weird accent—a hazard of being homeschooled by a family with members born anywhere from the twelfth century on.

Aunt Hyacinth's rooms were pretty much what you'd expect from a lady who still mourned Queen Victoria's death—and the fact that said queen turned down an offer of bloodchange.

I turned my attention back to my surroundings. My own imminent bloodchange not only made me unbearably sleepy, but it also made it really hard to concentrate. Aunt Hyacinth's parlour didn't help. And it was a parlour, not a sitting room or a living room. A *parlour*. I'd learned the difference before I'd learned to spell the word. With the proper British spelling, of course, for Aunt Hyacinth. I'd also learned medieval spelling for words in honor of Veronique—with a French flair in honor of her Aquitaine heritage—and modern English from Mom and Dad. It was a wonder I'd ever learned to spell my own name.

I sat in a brocade-cushioned chaise next to a huge copper urn filled with ferns. Aunt Hyacinth loved ferns; they'd been the fashion when she had her coming-out ball on her eighteenth birthday. She'd worn a white silk gown and made her curtsy to the queen. She'd taught me to curtsy and I'd taught Lucy, who had practiced until she gave herself leg cramps. The parlour had lace tablecloths on every surface and silver candlesticks and painted oil lamps and silhouettes in gilded frames. There was a small dressing room filled with corsets and petticoats and pointy boots. Lucy and I had spent hours playing in there when we were little. Lucy would still play in there, if Aunt Hyacinth would let her.

Aunt Hyacinth reclined dramatically on a velvet fainting couch, drinking her cherry-flavored blood. Mrs. Brown hopped up to curl by her feet, accepting slivers of rare beef as a mid-afternoon snack.

I wondered, not for the first time, if it was possible to be a vegetarian vampire.

"If you keep worrying so much you'll give yourself wrinkles," Aunt Hyacinth scolded me gently.

"I can't help it."

"Darling, your brothers survived the change. As a Drake woman, you are far stronger than they are. Just think, you'll wake up so refreshed. There's no feeling like it." She fanned herself with a silk fan decorated with white feathers. "And meanwhile, you ought to enjoy the courting."

"Courting? Aunt Hyacinth, they're drunk on my particular stink. And they don't care about me, they just want me to give them little fanged babies or whatever. And they want the power of the Drake name. Not exactly romantic."

She fanned harder. "But it can be, if you use it to your advantage."

"No thanks." I loved my aunt but there were certain topics we would never, ever agree on. Case in point: boys. Also: boyfriends, husbands, flirting techniques, and the supposed comfort of steel-boned corsets.

Aunt Hyacinth leaned over to run a hand over my hair. "It amazes me how beautiful you are sometimes, even with that loose, messy hair." Her expression was dark, fierce. I'd have been terrified if I didn't love her so much. "No harm will come to you, Solange, not while any of us live."

And that scared me most of all.

CHAPTER 6

◆

Lucy

Saturday afternoon

I left a note on the fridge door and snuck out, keeping the car in neutral until I was clear of the driveway. I knew they would have wanted to send someone with me, but I was incidental and I didn't want Solange to have one single minute of less protection because of me. Besides, I waited until the brightest and sunniest part of the day, and I only needed to make sure the cats had enough water and food. Everything else I needed was in town, in nice public crowded places or right on the Drake compound.

I knew Geoffrey would be in his lab now that he had a sample of the Hypnos powder. It really rankled that I'd been the weak link. Kieran had a lot to answer for, the jerk.

I drove to the last house on the compound and around to the

barn set out back. Geoffrey had been using it as a lab for decades. I knocked on the door before going in. It was a lesson I'd had drilled into me since I was old enough to know that it was okay to ignore certain explosions and black smoke out of this particular barn but that it was never okay not to knock. Geoffrey might hear my heartbeat approaching, but some of his experiments were delicate and dangerous and he wasn't always able to step away from them or close them down for visitor safety. And though I usually preferred Hyacinth's closet for my explorations, Geoffrey had helped me pass my biology exam last year and I was hoping he'd be as helpful today.

"Come in, Lucy," he called out, already sounding distracted. I'd have to make my questions short. The barn was outfitted with the most modern equipment, acres of counters and refrigeration units and at least a dozen fire extinguishers. Geoffrey was standing over a tray of beakers, wearing a creased lab coat.

"Hi. I know you're busy so I'll be quick," I said, wrinkling my nose at the familiar odor of formaldehyde and rubbing alcohol with a tinge of hay. There hadn't been hay stored in this barn for nearly a hundred years, but apparently that dusty smell never really went away. "Any progress with the Hypnos?"

"These things take time, you know that." He added a drop of blue liquid to a slide and slipped it under a microscope. "Just like I know that's not why you're really here."

"I'm sorry I let him get away."

He looked up. "It's hardly your fault—even I would follow orders if I got a mouthful of Hypnos. It's very potent, Lucy."

"I know."

"Now, what can I do for you?"

I bit my lip. "I want to know about the bloodchange."

"You know about the bloodchange."

"No, I don't. I know it's the big bad and everyone's freaked out, but that's it. And every time I ask Solange, she tells me not to worry."

"And she's right."

"Please." Apparently I wasn't above begging. "I just want to understand it so I can help."

He smiled gently. "Unfortunately, there's not much you can do to help, my dear. This is Solange's battle."

"Solange is my best friend," I said stubbornly. "So it's my battle too."

Something in my face must have convinced him I was going to make a nuisance of myself until I got what I wanted, because he finally sighed and said, "All right, Lucy. Have a seat."

I sat quickly, before he could change his mind.

"The bloodchange is still a bit of a mystery," he admitted. "I've been doing research and experiments to better understand our family's special challenge, but with varying degrees of success. It's not strictly scientific, nor is it strictly supernatural, so we have as many questions as answers. There are only a few other families who can procreate like we do. All other vampires are made, not born. Technically, the *Hel-Blar* are made the same way; it's only that they have a more violent transformation, without guidance or mentoring until it's too late."

"Are they as scary as everyone makes them out to be?"

"Yes."

"Do the Hounds get sick too?"

"In a manner of speaking, though not like us. Our change is genetic, you understand. As near as we can explain it, when our young reach puberty, the flux in hormones triggers the change. It's like the body attacks itself and then shuts down—until it is reawakened by drinking vampire blood. Our children need to be very strong to fight through it and win."

I swallowed. "But mostly everyone gets through it, right?"

"Mostly."

"Why do some go crazy? Is that a hormone thing, too? Like permanent PMS?"

He smiled briefly. "Not quite. It's just that some are stronger than others. The bloodchange is so difficult, some just can't hold on to themselves. If they get only just enough blood to survive, the thirst takes them over and it's all they can think about, like the *Hel-Blar*."

"Are you telling me Solange could turn into one of them if she's not strong enough?"

"I wish I knew for sure. The more likely outcome would be that she might simply die and not reawaken."

"This sucks." I scowled. "But Solange is totally strong enough. She won't die for real and she won't go crazy." If I said it enough, it would be true.

"I'm sure you're right," Geoffrey said soothingly. "She has strong genes, which is an asset. Drinking the blood from someone of the same lineage will restore her enough to win the battle. Her body won't attack the new blood, but it can't create its own supply either. At first, she'll need to drink every day to supplement, less as she gets older."

"She's not going to get older." I tried not to dwell on the fact that one day I'd be wrinkled and wearing dentures and she'd still look young enough to be my granddaughter. We had way bigger worries.

"She won't age physically, no. At least not for a few years, after her body completely adjusts to its new form. I'm afraid I don't really understand the science behind this adaptation yet. My theory is that it's another genetic survival mechanism: we reach our optimum age, where we look the strongest. It's a way to scare off predators, like making yourself look bigger to scare off a black bear."

"Oh. And her special pheromone thing is a survival mechanism too, right? How everyone's all obsessed with her?"

"Yes. It's a mating thing. Everyone is wondering if she'll be able to carry a vampire child to term."

"Gross."

"Study your Darwin, my girl."

As if. "One more thing, why are the *Hel-Blar* blue?"

"It's a side effect, like their fangs. Their extra fangs enable them to take their first . . . meals . . . with such violence and greed, it leaves them, in effect, engorged and bruised."

"Oh." I had to learn to stop asking these questions. I never liked the answer. I swallowed. "Thanks. I guess I should let you get back to work."

"Yes, Darwin's going to get a little help when I'm through." He turned back to his microscope and I knew he'd pretty much forgotten I was there by the time I reached the door. I didn't feel better exactly, but at least I didn't feel like I was the only one in the dark anymore.

I drove home, mind racing. My house seemed too quiet somehow, too empty. Mom's Kali statue watched as I put out several bowls of water. It had to last until my parents came back—just in case. It felt melodramatic to think like that, but I needed to be prepared. Solange would have been happy hiding out in some deserted cabin until this was all over, but I wanted to fight. My parents still didn't understand my violent tendencies considering the way I was raised: meditating, eating tofu, and taking long road trips in the middle of the school year to see petroglyphs or observe moose. My mom's rabid tolerance extends not just to people but all species—vampires included. Helena and my mom were best friends in high school but drifted apart when Mom went to college and then traveled around the world to find herself. It was ten years before Mom came back to her hometown. One night she went on one of her full-moon hikes and ran into Helena, who was pregnant with Solange and drinking the blood of a deer Liam had killed to help sate her cravings. Apparently, that kind of thing had only happened when Helena was pregnant with Solange and not any of her seven brothers.

Anyway, no amount of vampire mind control was going to make my vegetarian mom forget that particular sight. Helena couldn't hide from my mom, and their friendship was rekindled, which was how we came to be so close and comfortable with the Drakes. More comfortable than they were with us sometimes—case in point: Nicholas.

Nicholas.

I really wished he'd been a bad kisser. It would have been much easier to forget it ever happened, to not wonder if it might happen again.

"Focus," I told myself sternly, locking our front door, double-checking it. I watched every bush and tree suspiciously on my way back to the safety of my car. The tires squealed, sending up clouds of dust as I sped out of there. The back of my neck didn't relax completely until I'd reached the outskirts of town, with its candy-colored galleries and ice-cream parlors. The area was popular with artists, environmentalists, and homesteaders like my folks. There were few places with so much wilderness all around—dense forests and hidden waterfalls and even wolves, sometimes, singing on cold winter nights. The combination of the untamed countryside and the fact that everyone here was pretty private and accepting of alternative lifestyles made it a perfect place for vampires to live in undiscovered. At least I thought they were undiscovered. If not, no one talked about it. Folks here were far more likely to get heated over conspiracy theories and nuclear waste sites.

First, I stopped by the drugstore for nose plugs and I cleared them out entirely. The cashier didn't even blink. Then I went to the hardware store for hunting and camping supplies, which were big business in town. I felt a little silly, I admit, kind of like the comic book character I'd accused Kieran of emulating. But I was determined, too. If there was anything I'd learned from my parents, besides how to chop wood and prime the water pump, it was that you did what needed doing and you didn't complain about it or pretend it wasn't necessary. Afterward, I felt perfectly justified in rewarding myself with a double-shot cinnamon latte. And since my parents weren't there, I didn't even use soymilk. That was downright rebellious in our family. I nearly snorted—I was going back to a house where blood was sipped like a fine wine and vegetarianism wasn't exactly an option. I'd already made Solange promise she wouldn't drink any bunnies dry.

I was halfway back to my car when I felt the warning prickle. I swallowed, forced myself not to speed up or slow down, to keep my pace even and oblivious. There was a family eating hot dogs on a bench, someone else on a bicycle, two girls walking a tiny teacup Chihuahua. There was something else as well, that indescribable feeling of being watched, followed. I turned the corner, the green lawns of a park on my left, my car farther down on the right. No other pedestrians. The sun was making the sidewalk feel soft under my sandals. Almost definitely not a vampire then, it was too hot and bright.

There was the barest tremble from the hazel thicket. I wouldn't have noticed it at all if I hadn't been so paranoid about every single thing around me. Adrenaline shivered through me. I hoped I still looked like any other distracted girl, sipping my latte and juggling shopping bags. I waited until I was right next to the hazel before I chucked my latte and hollered, launching myself at whoever was skulking around back there. We went down in a tangle of flailing limbs and blistering curses. I saw black cargo pants, black nose plugs, black eyes. His code name was probably Shadow.

Kieran.

CHAPTER 7

♦

Solange

I went out back to my little shed. The sun was soft on the clapboard siding and the kiln tucked into the back. I did need my sunglasses but at least I didn't feel as tired as I had last night. I knew that when it came to me, my entire family went all overprotective and dramatic, so it was hard to know how many symptoms on their long list I could really expect.

I let myself into the studio and closed the door very deliberately. I wouldn't think about it right now. It never helped anyway. What did help was burying my hands in clay and the rhythmic spinning of my pottery wheel. It was dusty and quiet in here, just how I liked it. The long window offered the distraction of the wild fields and forest when I needed them. My tools and chemicals were stored in plastic tubs; the walls were fitted with wooden shelves all but groaning under the weight of bowls and cups and oddly shaped vases. Lucy kept telling me I should take my stuff into the gallery shops by the lake to sell it. It wasn't a bad idea. Though most of them did their business during the daylight hours, Lucy would make deliveries for me if I asked her to. It was something to think about.

If I survived my birthday, of course.

I scowled and attacked the clay. It was cool and obedient under my determined hands. I hated being frightened, almost as much as I hated being coddled. I worked until the sun was dipping slowly behind the trees. Geese flew overhead, honking. I wasn't any closer to figuring out Kieran Black or the bounty or how to give in gracefully to the bloodchange, but at least I was calmer. And possibly hungry again. I wiped my hands clean and went outside, inhaling deeply the fragrance of roses and wild mint. I was thinking so hard I wasn't paying attention to my surroundings.

First mistake.

I might not have super hearing yet, but the arrow whistled so close to my head I could hear the air through the fletchings. It thunked into one of the oak trees, showering splinters. At the same time, someone crashed into me, curling around me like a particularly heavy parka.

"Oof! What—"

"Get down, you ijit!" It was Bruno. He only slipped back into his native Scottish accent when he was really pissed off. "Get in the damn house." He ran me up the porch steps. I felt like the president of a small country under attack. All he needed was the ear transmitter and a pair of mirrored sunglasses. And a black suit—but I didn't think he'd ever wear a tie, even for us. He looked just like what he was: an ex-biker with a shaved head to disguise the balding, and tattoos from shoulder to knuckle. He'd been working for us since before I was born. Bruno shoved me inside and slammed the door behind us.

"Stay here," he barked, running back out, shouting orders into a walkie-talkie. The gardens were quiet; even the birds were cheerfully oblivious. My heart was thumping wildly, making me feel dizzy. That arrow had been really close, too close. And only one organization used wooden arrows of that style.

Helios-Ra.

I wondered if it had been Kieran, skulking in the shadows, waiting for me to turn my back. The sun glittered on the gravel drive, the black iron fence. No vampire ancient enough to withstand this kind of a summer day would be able to sneak onto the property. Someone would have scented his pheromones.

Bruno came back, eyeing me grimly. "The tunnels for you from now on, lassie."

"Did you get him?"

"Not even a damned footprint." He rubbed his head. "Get away from the window, Solange. It's not safe."

"This is getting ridiculous," I muttered.

"Agreed," he replied.

"I'm going to the loft," I told him peevishly.

"Use the tunnel," he repeated.

I went down into the basement and used the short passageway that linked the house to the garage. The second floor had been converted into training space complete with floor mats, punching bags, a weight machine, and two treadmills. The back wall was covered with fencing gear and swords. I didn't bother with the uniform or the mask since I was practicing on my own. I just needed the distraction. If pottery wasn't enough to really calm me down, lunging and stabbing an imaginary foe would have to do. I took up my favorite sword, or foil as it was called in fencing.

Out of habit I saluted my pretend opponent and bowed. Then I cross-stepped back and forward a few times to warm up. I lunged, I stabbed, I parried and circular parried and disarmed. I lunged again and again until my thigh muscles ached and sweat spiked my hair. I ducked right, I parried low, I jabbed high. Retreat, riposte, retreat, riposte.

I felt better until I happened to glance out the window and saw Bruno going back into the house, dragging a huge bag full of packages and flowers. I tossed my foil aside and sprinted down the steps, through the tunnel and up to the front hall. I scowled at the open bag, panting and scowling.

"What the hell is that?"

"More gifts, lass," Bruno said. "We're finding them all along the property line."

For some reason, all those presents were really pissing me off. I jabbed my hand inside and pulled out postcards, a clump of daisies, something that looked like a Ziploc bag full of blood.

"That's disgusting." I dropped it immediately. The light glinted off something silver and I pulled it out gingerly. It was an apple, perfectly crafted out of silver, with a leaf dangling from the stem. The delicate leaf was engraved with a name: Montmartre.

I put the apple aside so I could wipe my hands completely clean of Montmartre cooties, and it teetered on the edge of the table. It hit the floor, and the top opened on tiny hinges I hadn't seen. Blood poured out of the opening, thick and red. The coppery smell made me gag but I didn't have time to otherwise react. I was too busy staring out the front window.

"Where's Lucy's car?"

CHAPTER 8

◆

Lucy

"You asshole!"

I didn't think, just reacted with all the anger and guilt and worry I'd been carrying around all day. I punched him right in the nose. He reared back, grabbing his face.

"Shit, shit!"

"That's right, you sneaky bastard." I leaped to my feet, panting. "Use me against my best friend, will you?"

He reached into his pocket. I got to mine first, took out the pair of nose plugs I'd stashed there, just in case, and I shoved them in.

"Oh, no you don't," I snapped, smug as a cat with a mouthful of canary feathers. I was going to redeem myself, if I had to punch him ten more times to do it. My knuckles felt bruised, sore. Vindicated.

There was the teeniest, tiniest possibility my mom was right about my temper.

Kieran just blinked at me, bewildered. "Who taught you to punch like that?"

I smiled grimly. "The Drakes." He shifted, as if he was going to get up. "Uh-uh. You stay right there or I'll scream so loud half the town will come running. You might be part of some secret club, but I can still get you arrested for being a creepy stalker." I noticed the way he was trying to look at the back of my neck, and my wrists. "And what the hell are you doing now?"

"You don't have any scars."

"What?"

He pushed himself up so he wasn't sprawled in the dirt. His nose looked sore but I hadn't actually broken it. "Bloodslaves have scars, from the feedings."

"Don't use that word, it's insulting. And it makes me want to kick you. Hard."

He held up his hands, palms out, as he stood up fully. I took a step back, raised a fist. I could see the hilt of a knife in the top of his boot.

"You have to know that vampires murder people." I could tell he was thinking about his father. Sometimes it was a real pain that my own father had encouraged such a strong sense of empathy in me. He couldn't have taught me math?

"Kieran, humans murder all the time. And the Drakes aren't killers. They're not *Hel-Blar*, they know how to control themselves."

"They're all the same."

"Don't make me punch you again. My hand already hurts."

He nearly smiled. "You might be as scary as Helena Drake, one day."

"I intend to be."

"You're well on your way." He wiped blood off his face ruefully. A car passed by on the street.

"Leave them alone, Black."

"It's not that simple."

"It is *too*. Helios-Ra has a treaty or whatever, so stick to it."

"I'm a new agent. I only just turned eighteen. Do you really think I'm in charge over there? I have orders, just like everyone else."

"That's convenient," I sneered, gathering up my bags before turning away. "And totally lame." I stopped at the driver's-side door. "Don't be a lemming, Black."

◆

When I got back to the farm, one of the guards stepped out where I could see him and shook his head disapprovingly. Ooops. I was already flinching when I let myself out of the car and Nicholas opened the screen door. So much for sneaking out and then back in, none the wiser. Nicholas's nostrils actually flared.

"Lucky."

I flared mine back and felt like an idiot.

"Nicky."

I pushed past him, then wished I could go back out onto the porch to fight with him. I'd take that over Solange's pale, worried face any day.

"Lucy, are you okay?"

"I'm fine, Sol. I just needed supplies and to feed the cats." I dropped my bags, felt Nicholas come up behind me. She looked so relieved, it gave the guilt sharper teeth. No one else could make

me feel so bad without saying a single word. Bruno was doing a pretty good job though, looking like a disappointed parent before he went out to patrol.

"I'd have fed your bloody cats," Nicholas muttered. He saw my drugstore bags, looked at me incredulously.

"You went to buy lipstick? At a time like this?"

"Yeah, that's right, and an exfoliating mask. Don't be an ass. I went for supplies."

The sun filtered in through the window, and he flinched away, even though it was specially treated glass and he was in no danger. He looked tired enough to fall over. Even the shadows under his eyes had shadows.

"You should be in bed."

"I *was* in bed," he said pointedly. "Until you went shopping."

"I needed nose plugs." I lifted the pair hanging on a string around my neck. "And they've already come in handy."

He narrowed his eyes at me.

"Why?" He grabbed my wrist. "Why, Lucy?"

I tugged back but couldn't break his hold.

"Because." I stopped pulling. I'd only dislocate my own wrist. "I ran into Kieran Black. Literally."

They both stared at me.

"What?" Solange finally squeaked.

Nicholas turned my hand over. His eyes flared, went the color of frost, at the blood on my knuckles. I shrugged sheepishly.

"I nearly broke his nose." I half smiled. "I'll have to try harder next time."

He dropped my hand, stepped back. There was something fierce in his face, even when he smiled faintly.

"I guess I should be glad I'm not the only one you punch."

I made a face at him and dropped into a chair. I was starting to ache in muscles I didn't know I had. There were still roses everywhere, and the smell was overpowering.

"Did he hurt you?" Solange's face was stony.

"No, I'm fine." I watched Nicholas trying not to weave on his feet. He looked as if he were standing on a particularly wave-tossed boat. "Go back to sleep," I said with more gentleness than I'd planned. I paled when something occurred to me. "You didn't tell your parents, did you?"

"No," Solange said. "I only just found your note. I didn't even get a chance to tell Nicholas. He just stumbled out of his room, all freaked out."

We both turned to look at him. I thought he might be blushing—if vampires could blush, that was.

"The house smelled wrong," he muttered. He glared at us. "Shut up." Then he went up the stairs. I raised my eyebrows.

"He's getting weirder."

Solange snorted, pulled out a handful of nose plugs, air freshener sprays, and a bowie knife from my plastic bags.

"So are you."

◆

I waited until we were alone before I hustled Solange into her room.

"What are you doing now?" she muttered when I shut her door

and pressed my ear to the wood for a moment to make sure no one was listening. And by no one, I meant Nicholas.

"Okay, I should totally be a spy." I grinned at her. "All I need is some funky accent and I could be a Bond girl."

She groaned. "What did you do?"

"I stole this from Kieran, right after I punched him." I pulled out a small book from the inside pocket of my jacket. It looked innocuous enough, slender as a poetry chapbook, with a simple font and a sun illustration on the front cover. It was the title that stood out: *A Field Guide to Vampires*.

Solange read it, blinked, read it again, and then stared at me. "*A Field Guide to Vampires?* Is that a joke?"

I laughed out loud. "Nope. Just a little souvenir from the Helios-Ra." We sat on her bed and set the guide on the blanket in front of us. We skimmed the index, snorted at the pompous introduction and the pseudomedieval oath new recruits had to take. There was a bunch of stuff on hunter protocol that could come in useful someday. There was also a whole section on the Drake family, and a page devoted just to Solange, listing her stats, like she was a rare kind of frog one could search for in a swamp.

"It's kind of creepy." She made a face. "I'm starting to feel like the bearded lady at the carnival."

"I would never let you grow a beard," I assured her, trying to lighten the mood. If she hunched her shoulders any tighter, her collarbone would shatter. "I'm way too good a friend for that."

"Gee, thanks."

"All in a day's work."

"I can't believe they study us like that. I mean, did Kieran sit in a classroom and learn that I wear cargo pants and like pottery? And how do they know that anyway? And I'm not solitary, damn it, I just don't like crowds." She paused. "Okay, so maybe I am solitary, so what? And my nickname is *not* 'Princess Solange.' Give me a break."

I tugged the book out of her hands before she could twist it in half. It flipped open. "Hey, no way. I'm in here too."

Her eyes narrowed. "You are not."

"I totally am."

"Okay, that's going too far."

"Apparently, I'm brash and reckless." I snorted. "Better than being a mindless droid to some secret society." I did a double take. "Did you know one of my strengths is annoying Nicholas?"

She laughed despite herself. "Okay, that part's true."

"Shut up, he's the one who annoys me." I tapped the book thoughtfully. "Hmmm."

"Oh, God. That 'hmmm' is never good."

I ignored her and reached for the phone. "They know all about us, shouldn't we know a little about them too?"

"How? You can't just phone up a secret society."

"Maybe not. I mean, Kieran might not have a MySpace page, but he has to live somewhere, doesn't he? He's not like Black Ops or anything, right?"

"I guess not. Wait, what are you doing?" she asked as I dialed 411.

"Shh. Hello? Kieran Black in Violet Hill. Address unknown." I covered the mouthpiece. "I need a pen." She ran to her desk and practically threw one at me. I wrote on the back of the guide. "Thank you," I said before hanging up.

Solange and I smiled at each other, and it felt like the smile of two lionesses about to take down a gazelle.

I pushed each number as if I were squishing a bug. Kieran picked up on the first ring.

"Mom, for the third time, I've got the milk—"

"It's not your mom," I interrupted, smirking at Solange.

"Who is this?" he asked suspiciously.

"It's Lucy."

He made a very gratifying choking sound. "*What?* I never gave you my number."

"You're listed, genius. So you can add that to your little guidebook. I'm not only reckless, I'm resourceful too. And Solange isn't solitary, she just doesn't like you." She had a weird look on her face. "Are you okay?" I whispered to her. "Lie down." I could hear Kieran shuffling the phone, probably searching his pockets.

"You took my guide!"

"Yup. You want it back? Meet us tonight." Solange's eyes widened. I waved away her concern.

"I can get another guidebook," he told me.

"Yeah, but how would it look for a new recruit to have lost it to one of your profiles?" I had him there. "Besides, you owe me, Black." And there.

He sighed, like an old man. "I don't actually owe you, Hamilton."

"Do *so.*"

"Does Solange know you're doing this?"

Interesting. "Yes, she knows. Don't you think she's tired of playing monkey in the middle for you people? Ow, what?" That last part I said into the air since Solange had grabbed the phone from me, scratching me in the process.

"My nickname is not 'Princess,'" she said witheringly. "Fine. After sunset." Her voice hardened. "Come alone."

CHAPTER 9

◆

Solange

Saturday evening, sunset

That night every single one of my brothers was in a foul mood. My parents were worse.

"We have some leads," my father said tightly from where he stood by the fireplace. "Though not nearly as much as I'd like."

My mom was wearing her leather vest, the one with all the hidden compartments. Not a good sign. She only wore it for serious hunting or ass-kicking.

"Your father and I have to follow them, as will Hyacinth and your uncles." Aunt Hyacinth might have been off to track assassins, but she still looked stylish in her riding habit and jet cameo. Her only concession was a pair of pointy granny boots instead of silk dancing slippers. "Geoffrey is in his lab with the Hypnos sample. Ruby is . . . indisposed." Which was a polite way of putting it. "Bruno will patrol with his men." Mom looked at my brothers. "Every single one of you will stay here and look after your sister. Except for Sebastian, who's already left on an errand."

I gaped at her, horrified. "Mom, *no*." My brothers were insufferable enough as it was. Six of them duty bound to follow me would make us all crazy. Lucy cringed sympathetically.

Mom glanced at me. "Solange, you have to take this seriously."

"Mom, I *do*. You know I do. But you don't have brothers, you don't *know*."

Logan contrived to look offended. "We're wonderful brothers."

The others ignored me, nodding solemnly at our parents. I groaned. I was going to have to get Lucy to break all of their noses before the night was through. Good thing she'd had so much practice. It wasn't that I was ungrateful or didn't adore my brothers—it was just that Drake men were arrogant, unbending, and liberally laced with white-knight complexes, especially when it came to their baby sister. I watched my mom strap her scabbard on, the leather strap between her breasts, the sword at her shoulder. It made me feel small, frustrated, useless. I couldn't even Google bounties or Helios-Ra because I'd find nothing but gaming Web sites and bad movie clips. I admit I had already Googled Kieran, but nothing came up.

I followed them to the basement stairs. They'd take the underground tunnels that connected all the farms, with exits in the forest and out near the town, as well as farther into the mountains.

"Maybe you shouldn't go." I wouldn't be able to forgive myself if they were hurt on my account. Dad put his hand on my shoulder. He wasn't tall, but he had the solid, regal bearing of a medieval king.

"We'll be fine," he assured me, and I nearly believed him. I watched them go, feeling utterly wretched when I heard the heavy steel door clang shut. My brothers positioned themselves in a half circle around me, staring.

This was already a disaster.

"All right." Lucy shouldered her way to my side and made a waving motion as if they were annoying flies. "Shoo!" She narrowed her eyes. "I said shoo."

They dispersed, mostly startled into moving. Only Logan remained, leaning casually against the wall.

"Darling, I'm not some insect to be chased away."

"Darling?" She snorted amiably. "You're not ninety years old, either."

He straightened. "I'm charming," he informed her. "And women like endearments."

"Women know you just can't remember their names, but they like your pretty face enough not to care. Now give your sister some space before she short-circuits."

He winked at her before sauntering away. She winked back. I knew they were trying to keep the mood light for my sake.

"Thanks."

"You're welcome. You know how I love to boss your brothers around. Let's go upstairs."

I waited until we were safely ensconced in my room with the stereo playing loudly to cover our voices.

"How are we going to do this?" I asked. "I can't believe Mom and Dad sicced them all on me."

"It's okay, we can totally do this." She started to pace between my desk and the closet door. "We just have to keep them distracted somehow." She paused. "Connor will be on his computer all night. Maybe we could ask him to track Kieran down online, keep him busy."

"That'll definitely work. And maybe you could try convincing the others to watch a movie or something? Make it sound like I'm sulking and just want to be left alone?"

She nodded. "Brilliant. I'll be right back."

She wasn't gone long, and by the time she came back I could hear the sounds of some action movie on the television in the far family room. It was conveniently on the other side of the house from the sunroom, which had a door to the backyard.

"I made it really loud," she informed me proudly. "Logan looked a little suspicious but he's watching it. Connor's online and Nicholas was up in his room, so I thought it was probably safest to leave him there. If he's brooding, it could buy us some time."

I shook my head. "No amount of brooding or distraction will keep him off our trail."

She snorted. "As long as we act suspicious, he'll follow us for a while without saying anything and think it's his idea. Besides, it might be good to have a little vampire instinct on our side."

"You're kind of evil, you know that?" I grinned at her.

"I've been practicing," she shot back with her own grin. "So are you ready to do this?"

I nodded, pulling on a black sweater so I'd blend into the

shadows better. "You know this is definitely one of our dumber ideas?"

"Please, would you rather sit around here and worry?"

"Hell, no. Let's go."

"That's what I thought." She poked her head out the window. "I don't think we can climb down from here."

"Not without you falling on your head." I pulled her away. "I've seen you in gym remember?"

"Hey, you don't even go to my school."

"In that class you had at the park, that time you tripped on your shoelace and took out a row of girls in pink shorts."

"Oh." She made a face. "Right."

"We'll use the back stairs and go through the sunroom."

For some reason we had to stifle giggles as we crept down the stairs. I felt like I was in some bad silent movie. Lucy clutched my hand and we used the movie's car chase to cover our movements. My brothers were still young enough that they shouldn't be able to distinguish our heartbeats over that kind of volume, even if they thought they could.

The backyard was dark—we remembered to avoid the motion-sensor light. We stayed low, moved quickly.

"How do we know we can trust him?" Lucy worried, not sounding quite as confident and cavalier now that we were getting closer to the edge of the forest.

"I think we can." I didn't know why I thought that, I just did.

"Oh man, is it wrong that now I really hope Nicholas is following us?"

I shook my head mutely. I was kind of hoping the same thing.

Vampire hearing would be an advantage right now. We crouched in a thicket and waited. My palms were damp. Lucy fidgeted anxiously. Even the crickets sounded sinister.

The crack of a twig underfoot had us clinging to each other.

"Solange? Lucy?"

Lucy popped up, scowling. "You scared the hell out of me."

Kieran jerked back. "Likewise."

I stood up much more slowly, wondering why I felt shy. This totally wasn't the time. He looked at me for a long moment, then nodded. Lucy stared at him, then at me. If she said anything I was going to kill her. She pursed her lips but mercifully stayed silent, instead staring over his shoulder suspiciously.

"You don't have to do that," he told her. "I'm alone."

"Forgive me if I don't entirely trust your motives," she shot back grimly. "You tried to kill my best friend."

"I did not!" he exclaimed hotly. Lucy had the ability to make most guys revert to being ten years old. That should've been in their stupid field guide. "She wasn't even out in the garden."

"Technicality," Lucy grumbled. "You came for the bounty."

"Yeah. It's my *job*."

"You should get a new one. Your boss sucks."

"Here's your book," I said quietly, handing him the guide before they started to pull each other's hair.

"Thanks." Neither of us said anything else. I was starting to hope Lucy would snap at him again, when he finally glanced away. "Why'd you want to meet?"

"You have to know we didn't break the treaty."

"Look, like I told your mental friend here, I don't make the rules. I just graduated. And anyway, isn't it all part of your coup? To be queen?"

"Is that what they're telling you?"

"You don't *want* to be queen?"

"*No,*" I said emphatically. "I don't. Look, I'm the first girl born to the House of Drake. That's all. It's only a big deal because of people like you. I didn't ask for this."

"Then don't let them turn you into a vampire."

"Oh, sure, she'll just die instead," Lucy said waspishly. "Nice plan."

He blinked at me. "You really would? That's not a myth about the ancient families?"

"No, it's not a myth. And I really don't want my family being hunted because of me. Can't you do anything?" I wasn't sure why I was asking him for help; I only knew that we really had no other options. I had to do *something* and this was it. Problem was, he didn't look entirely convinced. "If you really believe we should be hunted down, why don't you just kill me now?" I took a step closer to him, opening my arms.

"Don't be stupid." He took a startled step back, as if I was the one covered in weapons.

"Why not? It's what you do, isn't it?"

"It's not like that. Besides, you're human. Mostly."

"For now. Does that mean you'll kill me after my birthday?"

"No! Maybe. I don't know. I just want to find the one who killed my dad."

"You were so convinced it was one of us." I stepped even closer, could see the way his pupils dilated.

"Solange," Lucy said nervously.

I didn't look away from Kieran. "So go ahead."

"What the hell do you think you're doing?" Nicholas stalked out of the woods, fuming. I was half-surprised smoke wasn't coming out of his ears. Kieran reached for one of the stakes on his belt.

"Don't," I said, stepping in front of him. "Please."

"Solange, get inside," Nicholas ordered through his teeth, forcibly lifting Lucy up off the ground and setting her out of his way when she tried to stop him. She clung to his arm like a monkey.

"We know what we're doing," she insisted, her feet dragging in the long grass. "Stop it, Nicholas."

"We won't bother you again," I told Kieran, and for some reason my voice came out sounding sad. I turned away from him. "Nick, let's go."

I marched across the field knowing Nicholas would follow me, no matter how much he wanted to hang around to punch Kieran.

I didn't look back to see what Kieran was doing.

◆

Logan was in the back garden when we got back to the house.

"I knew something was up with you two," he said, seething.

"They had a secret date with Kieran frigging Black," Nicholas informed him stonily.

"Oh, it wasn't like that," Lucy retorted. "Give me a break."

"What is *wrong* with you?" Logan's mouth dropped open. I pushed past him to go inside and then wished I hadn't. Quinn, Connor, Marcus, and Duncan were waiting in the sunroom, and each of them started yelling at once. Lucy winced, stepping up beside me.

"She's fine," she said. "She's fine!" She yelled at the top of her lungs. My brothers paused. The sudden silence was broken by a bell ringing from the basement. Quinn and Connor took off at a run. By the time we stepped into the hall toward the kitchen, they were already leading someone up the steps.

"London," I said in surprise. She was a distant cousin and we rarely saw her. She was slim and pale and looked just like her name, with black hair so sleek it always looked as if she'd been walking in the rain. There were silver studs in her ears, seventeen at last count, one in her nose, and another in her left eyebrow. She wore tight black clothing, as always. "What are you doing here?" I asked.

"You've been summoned."

"Our parents aren't here," I said.

"I know," she replied. "It's not your parents who've been summoned, only you."

"By who?"

"Madame Veronique."

I stepped back. "I don't want to go."

"You can't exactly refuse."

"Why does she want to see me?" Veronique never saw any of us before the bloodchange. Ever.

"Why do you think?" London's fangs were out, not because she was angry—she was always angry—but because she refused to be anything but what she was. She sneered at Lucy. It was a constant source of irritation that Lucy was mostly immune to her pheromones. "*That* has to stay here." London didn't approve of Lucy, never had. She thought mortals were too fragile for friendship, for the strength required to carry our secret. And she hated that she'd been every bit as mortal as Lucy before she was turned three years ago.

"As if I want to hang around you for a single second longer than absolutely necessary," Lucy snapped. I knew she was lying; she'd been desperate to get a look at Veronique for years now. Under the bravado and temper she was disappointed. Her pulse must have sped up, because London smirked. Nicholas licked his lips.

Marcus whistled between his teeth. "Bad luck, Sol. Veronique's terrifying."

Lucy stomped on his foot. "You're not helping."

"Why'd she send you?" Quinn frowned at London. "You're still one of Lady Natasha's ladies-in-waiting, aren't you?"

She nodded stiffly. Her divided loyalties were a sore spot with everyone. "I serve Veronique first, like everyone else in our family."

"That doesn't explain why she sent you."

"Because Veronique isn't the only one who's summoned Solange. Lady Natasha has too. Once Veronique heard Solange was being called to the royal court, she wanted the first visit."

"Crap." My eyes widened. "Both of them? Tonight?"

"Solange can't go now," Nicholas said. "It isn't safe."

London quirked an eyebrow. "You know as well as I do that it isn't a request. Just be grateful I was already in the area so Lady Nastasha didn't need to send one of her Araksaka boys." The Araksaka were feared. Every single one of them wore Lady Natasha's royal tattoo on their faces. They were her private army and answered only to her. Ever. And they were utterly ruthless about it; not only killing but torturing as well.

"Hell," Quinn muttered.

"Fine." I wiped my hands off on my pants. "Let's get this over with."

London shook her head. "You are *not* going dressed like that." I blinked down at my T-shirt and cargos, which only had one smear of dried clay on the cuff. "You'd be laughed out of the Hall. And Lady Natasha'd be insulted, having granted you a temporary reprieve from exile. Not to mention what Veronique would do."

"Shouldn't have exiled the Drakes in the first place," Lucy muttered.

"She had to, because of the prophecy. You wouldn't understand."

"Give me a break." Lucy visibly bristled at the disdain in London's voice. "I probably know more about your own history than you do. The prophecy was recorded during the reign of Henry the Eighth, after he cut off Anne Boleyn's head. Some old madwoman in Scotland went into a trance and babbled about a blood-born Drake woman ruling over the tribes, and when Solange was born you all freaked out about it, including Lady Natasha." She looked proud of herself. "See? I totally get it. Although, I don't get why she's not Queen Natasha instead of Lady Natasha? Wouldn't that make more sense?"

"She hasn't had a coronation," Logan explained. "She's technically not queen, because we technically don't have queens. We have autonomous tribes and civil wars and a love of tradition."

"So what's the big deal about Solange stealing her crown then? If it's all semantics?"

"The tribes are letting Lady Natasha play queen because she used to be part of the Host and she knows their ways. And she claimed power back in the twenties, before any of us were even born and a Drake daughter wasn't even an issue. Drake women were discouraged from court but not outright exiled until Solange was born."

"She sounds like a piece of work."

"She's the first to have ties strong enough even to hope to rule. She's kind of our best bet if we want to stop all the infighting and control the *Hel-Blar*."

"Until Solange," Nicholas added grimly.

"Exactly." Logan nodded. "Half the courts would defect to Solange if given the chance. Natasha might be our best bet, but she's also a power-hungry cow and still totally obsessed with Montmartre. Everyone knows that."

"I don't want her stupid crown," I muttered. I hated all this talk of prophecies and politics. As if I even *wanted* to be queen.

"Why didn't she exile *you* too?" Lucy asked London.

"I'm not really a Drake." London looked annoyed at having to answer the question.

"Are so." I frowned at her. She just shrugged.

"It's different for me. Anyway, you should be grateful for the exile. She could have just had Solange killed at birth, you know."

"And make her a martyr?" Connor asked. "Or draw Veronique out and have to deal with her wrath? Or have it look as if she might not believe herself to be the rightful queen after all?"

"She is the rightful queen," London insisted. She turned to me. "But *you're* the only Drake daughter born, not made."

"I know what I am, London."

"Well, then. Start looking the part."

"So now it's a fashion show, too?" I grumbled, following London and Lucy to my room. London went straight to my closet, made a face.

"Solange, honestly."

"What?"

"You can't wear any of this."

"She can wear something of mine," Lucy suggested. "I have better taste."

"Please."

Lucy, notorious for overpacking, pulled a dress out of her bag. It was more like a silk slip with lace on the hem and loops of beaded fringe she'd sewn to the straps. It was the exact color of red wine.

"It'll have to do," London said grudgingly.

I changed quickly, nerves fluttering in my belly. Dressing up like I was going to a high school dance was making me even more anxious. I put on a pair of Chinese slippers and the silver bracelet Hyacinth had given me last year.

My brothers lined up in the foyer, each wearing his best clothes. Sebastian was even wearing a suit. Logan was the only one who hadn't had to change. He was always stylish.

"You're not all coming with us," I said, pausing on the bottom step.

"Damn right we are," Connor said.

"What about Lucy? You heard what Mom said."

"I'll be fine," she said from behind me on the landing. "Don't worry about me."

I glared at my brothers mutinously. "We are not leaving her here alone."

Nicholas pushed away from the wall. "I'm staying."

"You don't have to," Lucy muttered.

"Good," I said, ignoring her. My mouth was dry. "Let's go."

CHAPTER 10

◆

Lucy

The very second the door closed behind them, Nicholas started shouting. I guess I shouldn't have been surprised.

"I can't believe you did that!" he railed. "After the field party, the vamps in the garden. Didn't you hear a single word I said?"

"No, why don't you yell a little louder?"

"This isn't funny, Lucy."

"I never said it was." I crossed my arms and watched him stomping furiously around the foyer. "We did what we had to do. It was worth a try."

"He could have killed her. And you." He slammed his hand down on a side table, dislodging a vase of roses. It fell to the floor, cracking on the marble. Water and rose petals clung to his boots.

"But he didn't." The truth was I was still feeling the adrenaline.

I curled my hands into fists so he wouldn't see the way they were trembling. Maybe I wasn't made for this spy stuff after all. "And anyway, you went out there and fought a bunch of pheromone-crazed vamps and we didn't lecture you."

"It's not the same."

"Right."

"For one thing, I'm a lot harder to kill than you two."

It was hard to argue with that. "Well, whatever," I mumbled lamely.

We glowered at each other for a while longer. For the first time, I could really see the worry etched around his eyes and the way his mouth tightened. He wasn't just pale, he was faintly gray. We must have really scared him. I tried to imagine what he'd felt seeing his baby sister and her best friend in the woods at night with a Helios-Ra hunter. I sighed. "As much fun as it is to stand around here yelling at each other, do you think maybe we could do something else for now?"

He jerked his hand through his hair. "It's pretty late. You could go to bed."

"Are you kidding?" I stared at him. "Like I could sleep."

"It'll be hours before we hear anything."

I bit my lower lip. "Is Veronique really that scary?"

He looked up, nodded once. "There's just something about her."

"She wouldn't hurt Solange, would she?"

"No, she's really big on family and tradition and all that. It's the royal courts I'm worried about."

"Did you reach your parents yet?"

"No."

"Crap."

"Yup."

"Well, we can't sit around here worrying all night. I have to do *something*."

"Why don't you call up another vampire hunter for tea?" he suggested drily. He looked calmer though, less like he was clenching his jaw so hard he'd snap off a fang. "How did you manage that, anyway?"

"I called the operator. His number was listed."

"Seriously?"

"And I picked his pocket." I preened like a peacock.

Nicholas shook his head, grinning that rare crooked grin that made my stomach flutter. "You didn't."

"I totally did. And I found this Helios-Ra handbook guide to vampires. I guess all the recruits get a copy. I was even in it; I'm a Person of Interest. Go me."

I thought he'd get a chuckle out of it, but his face went so cold I had to stop myself from shivering.

"What?" he asked with deadly calm. "Helios-Ra has targeted you?"

I shook my head enthusiastically. "No, nothing like that, don't worry. It's just a profile page. Solange had one too." His jaw clenched again. Oops. Shouldn't have mentioned that. God, maybe he was right. I do have a big mouth. I tried a soothing smile. "Really, it's okay. Anyway, we made photocopies of everything on Sol's printer. And we had Connor doing his computer geek thing before London dropped in to be her usual sunny self." I tilted my head. "Your computer's faster than Solange's laptop. Think we could find something on the bounty or Helios-Ra? Anything?"

He looked thoughtful. "It beats sitting around here waiting. Connor's the one with the Internet mojo though, not me."

I shrugged. "Worth a try." Anything to fill the time, because otherwise I was going to bounce between worrying about my best friend and wondering when her brother got so freaking hot. Neither of those appealed to me as a sane pastime.

We went up to the attic floor, which had been converted into seven bedrooms, two bathrooms, and a sitting room—all without a single window anywhere. Nicholas's room was the smallest; there was space only for a bed, a dresser, and his desk. I had to sit on the edge of the bed since there was no other chair. It was only half-made, with a navy blue blanket. The last time I'd been up here there had been pirate sheets and wooden swords.

I looked around curiously. There was an iPod dock and stacks of music magazines and clothes in a pile in the corner. There was also a small photograph on his nightstand. It was of the two of us on my fifteenth birthday. I was laughing, the light glinting off my glasses and the sequins on my scarf, and Nicholas was turned toward me, with serious eyes and a half grin. I touched the frame.

"I've never seen this picture," I said quietly. I kind of wanted to ask him if I could get a copy, but I didn't want to sound sappy. He looked over his shoulder from where he was booting up his computer.

"It's . . ." He grabbed it, stuffed it into the top drawer of his desk. "It's nothing."

Liar. Still, even though I knew it wasn't nothing, I didn't know what it actually meant, either. It was probably no big deal. I shouldn't read into it. I couldn't help smiling, though.

"Stop that," he muttered, not even looking up from the keyboard. I smiled wider. "I mean it."

"So how do we find and infiltrate the database of a secret society?" I asked.

"I have no idea."

I scooted to the edge of the bed so I could see what he was typing. "Hey, you do have some mojo," I said approvingly. The screen was a garble of HTML codes. "I can't even read that."

"Don't get too excited," he warned me. He typed for a bit, waited, typed some more. I watched, got bored, lay back on the bed, and stared at the ceiling. He put music on, choosing some of my favorite bands. He typed some more. I felt my eyes drifting shut despite myself.

"Think your boyfriend would mind the photo?" he finally asked quietly, so quietly I barely heard him.

That woke me up. "What boyfriend?" I sat up. "I have a boyfriend now?"

"Jett or Julius or whatever his name is."

"Julian?" I blinked, confused. "You're way out of the loop. Julian dumped me during exams. Well, actually, he didn't even really dump me. I just found him with his tongue in Jennifer King's mouth."

"You don't sound torn up about it."

"Please, it was forever ago. I called him names, and then when I got home I realized I didn't actually care. I didn't even bother with the requisite breakup hot fudge sundae."

"Oh."

I didn't know what to do with this Nicholas. It felt like we were about to have a moment. We'd never really had a moment. Okay, we'd had that kiss—make that two kisses. But they weren't real, were they? The first was in the interest of subterfuge, the second a scientific test of my immunity to pheromones. I swallowed, suddenly nervous. I hadn't been expecting a moment.

"Got something."

Which was for the best because I clearly wasn't going to get one. I tried not to feel disappointed.

"What did you find?" I asked, pretending my voice hadn't squeaked.

"I'm not sure yet but it's got more security than I've ever seen." He frowned. "I can't crack this. I'm not even sure Connor can."

"But he has a place to start, right?"

"I guess. For what it's worth." He pushed away from the desk.

"We had to try."

"Yeah." He didn't look pleased. I nudged his foot with my boot.

"Want to crank call Kieran?"

He sat next to me, smiling. "Maybe later. Nothing gets you down, does it?"

"Sure it does." He was close enough that his knee brushed mine. "When this is all over I'll have myself a good cry and a pity-party. Right now, I just don't have the time."

"You're kind of amazing."

I looked at him out of the corner of my eye, flushing. It was odd to get a compliment like that from him. And really nice. "Solange says I'm kind of evil."

"That too."

"Can I ask you a question?"

"Sure," he replied warily.

"Were you scared during your bloodchange?"

He stilled. "Yes."

"Did it hurt?" I couldn't stand the thought of Solange suffering. It wasn't fair. She was too good a person to go through all of this.

"Some. Mostly I just felt weak and exhausted, like I had a really bad fever. By the time I lost consciousness I didn't really care anymore. I was too tired."

I was sorry now that I'd been locked out of the house, that I couldn't have been there for him. I could easily picture him writhing in pain on this bed, soaked in sweat, delirious. "Geoffrey says it's kind of like a battle."

"It is. It feels like you're hallucinating though and even now it's hazy. I'm not sure what was real and what wasn't."

I touched his knee. "I'm sorry I brought it up."

"Don't be."

"Solange is really strong," I said it again. "Stronger than everyone thinks she is."

"I know."

"What got you through?" I whispered. "Do you remember?"

He nodded but wouldn't look at me. When he didn't elaborate, I turned to face him. "What? Is it a secret? Don't I know all the deep dark Drake secrets by now?"

He shifted uncomfortably. "I guess."

"What then?"

"You."

I swallowed, stunned. "Me?"

"Yeah." He stood up and went to the door, where he paused for the barest second. "You got me through."

CHAPTER 11

◆

Solange

I was not enjoying this.

We weren't even there yet and I just wanted it to be over.

We didn't take the tunnels to Veronique. Her house outside of Violet Hill was completely independent of the Drake compound and Natasha's royal courts in the caves and pretty much everything else. The house was perched on a hill and painted dark gray, with Victorian gables and stunted thorn trees all around. It was straight out of Wuthering Heights.

"I can't believe she came here for this," I muttered as Marcus turned into the lane. It was miles before it wound through the woods and then out onto a clearing with a narrow driveway. "She never comes here."

"You're special," Quinn told me. "She came here for you."

"Great."

We got out of the car and I tried not to compare the slamming of the doors to gunshots. Everything had a dark, final feel here. I shook it off. I was letting the melodrama of the house infect me. This was technically my great-great-several-times-great-grandmother. While I doubted she'd baked me cupcakes, I had to assume she didn't mean me any harm either. Each of my brothers had survived the formal introduction. I would too. I kind of wished Lucy was here; I could have used some of her swagger. I'd just have to find my own.

"Come on, little sister." Duncan nudged me up onto the porch. The door swung open before we could knock. Veronique didn't have guards, but she did have ladies-in-waiting. The one who answered the door didn't betray a flicker of emotion. She was dressed in a suit with a pencil skirt and wore her hair scraped back into a bun. She looked competent and about as warm as winter at the top of a mountain.

"You're expected," she said. "Come in." She stepped aside. "I am Marguerite."

We bustled into the foyer and then just stood there in a hesitant clump. Even Logan wasn't flirting with her. London scowled but looked at the floor. There were chandeliers everywhere, made of jet and crystal drops. Oil lamps burned on wooden chests serving as tables. It smelled vaguely like incense. A shield with the Drake family crest hung on the wall with our motto: "*Nox noctis, nostra domina*," which translated roughly to "Night, our mistress."

"Only Solange was summoned," Marguerite murmured disapprovingly. "The rest of you may wait here." She pointed to a long church bench. My brothers sat obediently, without a word. That was enough to scare me, even without the whole matriarch thing. "You"—she turned to me—"may follow me."

I took a deep breath and trailed her down the hallway. There were several doors leading into drawing rooms and parlors and a huge dining room. She ignored them all and went straight back to a set of French doors, opened up into a long ballroom with polished parquet floors and tapestries on the wall.

"Madame." Marguerite bowed her head. "She has arrived."

Veronique sat on one of those curved padded benches that were in every medieval movie I'd ever seen. She wore a long blue-gray gown with intricate embroidery along the hem and trailing bell sleeves. Her hair was hazelnut brown, her eyes so pale they were nearly colorless, like water. She was so still, she didn't look real. There was something definitely not-human in her face. I swallowed convulsively. I was so nervous I thought I might throw up on her. When she moved, just an inch, I jumped.

"*Mon Dieu,*" she murmured in a voice as distant and mysterious as the northern lights. "Your heart is like a little hummingbird."

"I'm sorry." I wasn't sure why I was apologizing, only that it seemed best. Some instinct inside me trembled, like a rabbit under the shadow of an eagle. For all her porcelain beauty, she was a predator.

"So you are Solange Drake," she said, considering.

"Yes, Madame." I curtsied, putting every detail Hyacinth had painstakingly taught me into it. This was no courtesy bob a la Jane Austen; this was a full court curtsy. I stepped my right foot behind my left and bent my knees out and not forward. I went as low as I

could without toppling over or sticking my butt out. I bent my head slightly. I prayed really hard that she'd be impressed.

"Very good," she said. "You may rise."

I stood back up and wobbled only a little. *Thank you, Aunt Hyacinth.*

"I am gratified to know your family has taught you proper etiquette."

"Thank you, Madame." Could she tell I was starting to sweat? It was hard to just stand there under her scrutiny. She was so composed, so hard.

"I understand Lady Natasha has summoned you to her court."

"Yes, Madame."

"She is not to be trusted, that one."

"No, Madame."

"You know the prophecy, of course."

I nodded.

"We've been waiting a long time for a girl to be born to us."

Great, no pressure.

"Your bloodchange is fast approaching. I can smell it on you. Even frightened as you are, your heart beats slower than it ought to."

I wondered if that was why I felt like I might pass out. I lifted my chin. I was not going to embarrass myself or my family.

"I would have you strong enough to survive, little Solange. I may not want the royal courts for my own, but I won't have them taken from our family as if we are nothing."

She picked up a long silver chain from the small table beside her. The vial on the end was clear, capped with silver and held with

more silverwork, curled to look like ivy leaves. "Do you know what this is?"

"No, I don't." She held it up. From this angle I could see the vial held a dark red liquid inside. "Oh. It's blood."

"My own, to be precise." She twirled it once. I watched it, mesmerized despite myself. "I do not share my blood lightly—only in extreme circumstances, you understand."

I didn't understand actually. But if she made me drink that, I really would throw up on her.

"I am prepared to give this to you. When your birthday arrives, drink it and it will give you the strength you need to claim your legacy."

This probably wasn't a good time to tell her I didn't want to be queen.

"Your brothers didn't need it; the Drake men have been turning for centuries. But you're different. I am curious to see how this will play out, and precious little incites my curiosity these days."

So maybe being the bearded lady at the carnival wasn't so bad after all.

"You will, of course, have to prove yourself worthy."

"Of . . . course." Because just handing it over would be too easy. "How do I do that?"

"There are skills every Drake woman should know, to honor her heritage. We will begin with embroidery."

My mouth hung open. "Embroidery?" I sucked at embroidery. Aunt Hyacinth had tried to teach me, but we'd both given it up as a lost cause. Lucy, strangely, had picked it up really quickly and embroidered a tapestry of Johnny Depp as Jack Sparrow for my

last birthday. Somehow, I didn't think that was going to help me right now. "I'm afraid I'm not very good at embroidery."

Her lips pursed. My palms went damp. Her fangs were out, as pointed and delicate as little bone daggers. "That's disappointing, Solange."

I was going to die because I couldn't embroider roses on a pillow. "I'm sorry," I whispered.

"Can you draw?"

"A little. I can throw pots. I don't suppose you have a kiln?"

"No, but duly noted." She waved her hand and suddenly Marguerite was back. I hadn't seen her leave, and I hadn't seen her return. She was carrying a small table like it weighed nothing and a chair. She set them down in front of me, then produced a sketchpad and pencils. "Go on," Veronique murmured. "Draw me something."

I wiped my hands and reached for a pencil, eyes racing over my surroundings for a subject. If she asked me to draw her, I might as well kill myself right now. I noticed a clay vase in the corner, holding a bouquet of stakes. I drew vases and pots all the time, getting ideas for my work at the pottery wheel.

I broke the tip of the first pencil. I took another one but had to wait until the tremor in my fingers subsided before trying again. This time I drew lightly, trying to pretend that my future didn't actually depend on it. Veronique glanced at my page.

"Passable."

I let out a breath in a big whoosh. She was like the scariest teacher ever. It made me glad I'd never gone to a regular school.

"And now for music. The harp? Piano?"

The harp? Was she serious? My mother taught me how to avoid hunters, shoot a crossbow, and stake a rabid vampire at twenty paces, not how to play "Greensleeves."

"I . . ."

She rose from her chair with the speed of an ancient vampire and the grace and posture of a prima ballerina.

A prima ballerina who was about to pass judgment on me.

"No music at all?" She did not sound pleased. I stumbled back a step before deciding to hold my ground. I'd been telling Lucy for years not to run because it only made vampires chase you. "Tell me, what *can* you do?"

I felt useless and insignificant. And I couldn't think of a single thing I could do that might impress her. How did you impress a nine-hundred-year-old vampire matriarch?

"Math?" she snapped.

"Yes," I replied, relieved. "I'm good at math."

"History?"

"Yes."

"When was the Battle of Hastings?"

"1066."

"Who was Eleanor of Aquitaine's first son to rule?"

"Richard the Lionheart."

"What year were my twins born?"

"1149."

"Can you fight?"

"Yes."

"With a sword?"

"Yes."

"Show me."

She clapped her hands once and another woman walked in, wearing the traditional white fencing uniform and face guard. I could tell by her eyes, which were light green, that she was a vampire. I had no idea if she was a Drake. And though I was pretty good at fencing, how was I supposed to beat a vampire? I was still human, and it was late enough that I would have been yawning by now if I'd been any less scared. My opponent gave me a mask and a vest and a foil.

"Begin," Veronique demanded before I'd even had a chance to test the balance of the blade in my hand.

We began.

I gave the proper salute, bringing my handle up to eye level and bowing. My opponent did the same. Then she lunged. I cross-stepped backward, blocking her attack. The slender blades scraped together. She lunged again and I used a circular parry, low this time. I didn't touch her, not once. She was too quick, a blur of white. I'd never felt slower. I was at a distinct disadvantage but I kept going.

"*Riposte!*" Veronique hissed, and I obeyed, cross-stepping forward to attack. I blinked sweat out of my eyes.

She blocked me, feinted, and then brought her sword down toward my head. I held up my own sword, parallel to the gleaming floor, and absorbed the power of the blow in my arms. The force of it rang through my bones. I knew if she'd wanted to, she could have cleaved me in half.

"Enough," Veronique called out, sounding satisfied. I lowered my arms, panting. There was the sound of footsteps in the hall and then my brothers all trying to race through the door at the same time.

"Solange!"

"Are you hurt?"

When they realized I was unharmed, they stopped together, mouths snapping shut. Their eyes went from me, to Veronique, and then they bowed in unison.

"*Bien*," she said to me. "You may go."

I took off my mask and left it with my foil on the floor. I was halfway to the door in my haste to get out of there when she stopped me. "Solange."

I nearly groaned. "Yes, Madame?"

"Don't forget this." She moved so fast I didn't see her, but she was suddenly standing next to me. Even my brothers looked startled. She handed me the vial. I slipped the chain over my head.

"Thank you."

CHAPTER 12

◆

Lucy

Nicholas lounged in that irritating way of his, reading through the photocopy of the field guide. He glanced up, watching me pace back and forth, back and forth. "I had no idea you were so fitness conscious."

I paused. "What?"

"Well, you *are* doing aerobics in the middle of the night."

I hadn't realized my pacing had practically turned into a jog. My breath was a little short, my leg muscles vibrating with tension. He was holding himself very carefully, as if he might break apart. Or as if I might. I made an effort to calm my pulse, dropped onto the sofa, and tried to sprawl as irritatingly as he did, but I couldn't just sit there waiting. I piled kindling in the hearth and lit a fire. It was too warm outside for one, but I needed something to do. Nicholas's fists unclenched.

"I hate this," I said as the flames caught. It wasn't nearly enough to distract me.

"I'd never have noticed. You hide your feelings so well." His grin was crooked. It made him look nearly approachable, warmed by that unearthly beauty. Solange was the only scruffy Drake I'd ever met, and I didn't know if she'd suddenly start wearing dramatic gowns after her birthday.

"Really, *really* hate this," I added. The gardens were dark behind the treated glass. Or so I assumed, since we'd pulled all the curtains shut, just in case. It made everything cozy, romantic. "We should never have let her go," I said.

"Bossy as you are, Solange doesn't take orders from you."

"I can't think why, the Drakes are so malleable." I sat up straight as something occurred to me. "Hey, you have the key to the vault."

"Do I?"

"Yes, you do," I told him pointedly. "And I want a stun gun."

"It's not a department store."

I got up, tugged on his hands. They were cool to the touch. I pulled harder, before letting myself get distracted. "Come on."

He made a big production of sighing like I was crazy, but at least he followed me down the stairs and through the halls, some of which doubled back on themselves, toward the family vault. It was more of a safe really, with a secret tunnel exit, oxygen, blood supplies, and weapons. I'd never actually been inside before. I bounced on my heels impatiently. He shook his head.

"You're acting like we have Santa locked in there."

I rubbed my hands together.

"This is better than some old fat guy. Now gimmee."

His glance was dry. "You're not even supposed to know where this door is."

"Please. I know every corner of this house, including the dirty magazines Quinn keeps under his bed." I tossed my hair back smugly. "Helios-Ra has nothing on me. Rat bastards." I knew I was starting to babble, even for me, but I had to keep my body from reacting to his closeness. I should have been immune to his pheromones. I must have been more tired than I'd thought.

He unlocked the door, angling his body so I couldn't see if he was using a key or a numeric code. He probably knew that if I actually saw what the key looked like, I'd try and steal it. The door swung open silently, heavily, and he switched on the lights, which flickered briefly before glinting on a wall of steel shelves lined with boxes of arrows and stakes and cases of bullets. Guns were securely hung on a steel rack next to swords and claymores and axes on iron hooks. I let out a reverent breath. Nicholas shook his head at my avarice.

"This was a bad idea."

I lightly touched a wicked-edged blade.

"It's even better than I thought." There were baskets of quarter-staves and fighting clubs and spears. "Where are the stun—oooh. Shiny." I reached for a crossbow, turning to grin at Nicholas. He swung backward, bending to get out of arms' reach in a way that would have snapped a human spine in half. His dark shirt fluttered like wings. I lowered the crossbow, rolling my eyes.

"Stop it."

He straightened. "We all remember what you almost did to Marcus."

"That was two years ago." I grabbed a quiver of wooden arrows that looked more like stakes. "I'm taking this one."

He frowned. "No, you're not. And why?"

I frowned back. "Hello? Bounty hunters? Helios-Ra? The walking undead? Pick one."

"No one's going to hurt you."

"Not with this thing in my possession." I propped the crossbow against my shoulder. It was surprisingly light. He looked as if he wanted to argue but changed his mind. I was instantly suspicious. There was nothing he loved more than to argue with me. We'd been honing our skills on each other for nearly a decade. Instead he opened a carved wooden chest that looked as if it belonged in a pirate movie. He pulled out a silver chain, with thick, old-fashioned links.

"Here, put this on." He tossed it to me.

I caught it seconds before it collided with my nose.

"What is this?" A cameo roughly the size of a dollar coin hung on the chain. It was carved with the Drake family insignia, a dragon with ivy leaves in its mouth, symbols of strength and loyalty, respectively. It was beautiful, accented with a single teardrop jet bead. "How come I've never seen these before?"

"Your parents probably have one, but they've never really needed to use it."

I held it up to the light.

"Why, is it magical or something?" I rattled it gently, waiting for something weird to happen.

He smiled at me. It was kind of unusual for him but not quite the magical event I'd been hoping for.

"Not really." He nudged me to turn around so he could work the clasp. His fingers were light and cool on the back of my neck. For some reason I had to stop a delicate shiver. "There." His voice seemed husky. It tickled my ear. "This will keep you safe. It marks you as one of us. Vampires or the Helios-Ra would recognize this and know that to take you on would be to take on the entire Drake clan."

I touched the pendant briefly. "Thanks."

"Of course, I wouldn't flaunt it until I knew for sure I wasn't dealing with a bounty hunter." He paused. "On second thought, maybe you shouldn't wear it." He held out his hand, as if he wanted me to take it off. I took a step back, clutched it protectively.

"No way." The lights flashed twice. I frowned at them. "Power surge?"

"Silent alarm. Someone's here."

We both rushed toward the door, nearly getting stuck, like some bad sitcom episode.

"Stay behind me," he snapped. His eyes were eerily pale. The weight of the crossbow was reassuring in my hands as we crept up the stairs. "And try not to shoot me in the back with that thing."

"Yeah, yeah."

When we reached the top, he paused, nostrils flaring. The front door shut quietly.

"Uncle Geoffrey." Some of the tension leaked out of his stance. I lowered the crossbow.

"I didn't know your sense of smell was that particular," I said. "I just thought you could tell if it was vampire or not."

"Everyone has a scent. If you're around them long enough, you kind of catalogue it." He didn't look at me. "You smell like a blend of pepper and cherry bubble gum."

"I do?"

Before I could press him further, he stepped out into the foyer, where his uncle was setting down a cardboard box.

"More gifts for Solange," he said drily. "Bruno's been through and scanned the bunch. Careful," he added when we bent for a closer look at the jumble of packages, wrapped in everything from brown paper to silver tissue. The lumpy envelope on top had a brownish stain leaking through. "That one's a cat's heart," Geoffrey said calmly.

"Ew." I recoiled. "What? Ew!"

"A gift." He shrugged, unconcerned. "It's considered a delicacy in some of the more remote tribes."

"Okay, gross . . ."

"That one's a kitten's. A love letter, I imagine."

"A kitten?" I stared for a full ten seconds, my mouth hanging open. I only managed to close it to swallow the threat of bile. "A kitten?"

"Uncle Geoffrey." Nicholas winced. The family dogs raced over to see why I was shrieking.

"Sorry. Sometimes I forget she's not fully one of us."

Later, I'd feel flattered by that. Right now I was mad. Way too mad.

"Is there a return address? Who sent that? I'm going to kick his ass." I had to turn my back on the package. "I'm not happy about this. Seriously."

"We got that," Nicholas said. There was something weird about his expression. His jaw was clenched so tightly I wondered why his teeth didn't pop right out.

"What's the matter with you?" I asked.

"Nothing."

"Nicholas, you just bent your ring, you're clenching your fists so hard."

"It smells like candy."

"What does?" I asked, confused. "What are you talking about?"

He glanced at the stained envelope. "It's still covered in blood."

"You are not serious." He nodded once, as if it was the hardest thing he'd ever done. "That's disgusting," I told him. "Seriously."

"I know."

"Okay then."

We went into the huge living room, where his uncle was already busy at the library end, pulling books off the oak shelves. Then he sat down at the table. Lamps burned behind ruby glass. Byron, the oldest Bouvier, licked my fingers, sensing my lingering agitation. Seeing vampires drink blood or snap each other's necks and crumble into dust was different than craving kitten hearts. That was just too much.

"Easy," Nicholas murmured. Geoffrey glanced at us.

"Lucky, sit down, your heart's racing. If it goes much faster, you'll pass out."

"She's still mad."

"She can be mad sitting down."

I sank into one of the chairs, leaning my elbows on the wide table, the same weathered oak as the shelves.

"Has your aunt Hyacinth come home yet?"

Nicholas shook his head. "You're the first."

Geoffrey frowned. "Am I?"

"Why?"

"She's not answering her phone or her pager. Hmm. Well, never mind, I'm sure she's fine." He looked around. "Where's Solange? Is she asleep?"

Nicholas sat next to me. "She's not here. She was summoned by Lady Natasha."

"What?" Geoffrey was on his feet so fast he blurred around the edges. "Why?"

"London wouldn't say, or more likely didn't know. If she *had* known, she'd have bragged about it." Nicholas frowned at his uncle's reaction. "And she wouldn't have come to fetch Solange if there was any real danger."

"She's rather dazzled by royalty, my boy." Geoffrey closed his eyes. "Damn." He reached for his phone. "We know who set the bounty, Nicholas." He pressed a button and the number dialed itself quickly.

"Who?"

"Lady Natasha."

CHAPTER 13

◆

Solange

We left the car just inside the property line of Geoffrey's house and used his tunnel access. The tunnels smelled of damp and smoke from the torches in the lesser-used parts of the corridors. It was very quiet—there were only soft footsteps and my ragged breathing. It was the safest route to Lady Natasha's royal court. She stayed in the mountains during the summer months in a complicated cave system. She traveled the rest of the year between her different holdings, like a medieval queen. Our town is considered her summer retreat, simple and countrified but relaxing enough for the odd week or two. And everyone knew the real reason Lady Natasha had chosen to come here was to keep an eye on our family.

"Are you sure she didn't say anything else?" I asked London.

If Lady Natasha expected me to embroider or dance a waltz, I damn well wanted a little notice this time.

London shook her head. The flickering light glinted off her tight leather pants. "She's a good queen, Solange. You don't have to worry."

"London, in case you failed to notice, there's a bounty on all our heads. Yours included. And our side of the Drake family has been exiled for years."

She shrugged one shoulder negligently, though I did see her hand tighten. "It's not the same for me. I was turned, I wasn't born into the Drake family."

"Your dad married your mom and then he turned you on your twenty-first birthday. I'd say that makes you a Drake."

"Whatever."

"It's no different than our dad turning our mom after Solange was born."

London shrugged again. It was starting to get on my nerves. We couldn't all be as blasé as she was. Some of us were going to be very grounded by morning. And by some of us, I meant me.

"Mom and Dad are going to freak," I muttered, stumbling into Logan. "Oof."

He steadied me. "Careful. You'll wrinkle the velvet."

Connor stopped as well, in the lead. He held up a hand.

"Someone's coming."

"Stay close to me." Logan's fangs elongated, gleaming wetly.

"It's probably just an honor guard," London whispered. "Lady Natasha's big on ceremony."

Quinn shook his head, nostrils flaring. "I don't think that's it."

"You're overreac—"

Vampires raced down the hall toward us, some scuttling on the walls like giant ants. Every hair on the back of my neck stood up. Maybe they weren't *Hel-Blar*, but they were warriors; either sworn to Lady Natasha or seeking the bounty for killing us. Connor, Quinn, and Marcus formed a front line of defense, and Logan and Duncan circled around to guard our backs. London and I stood in the middle. I took the stake she handed me. I didn't have anywhere to keep a weapon in this stupid borrowed dress. I wouldn't make that mistake again. Adrenaline flowed through me, making my fingers tremble slightly.

The hissing rolled over us, crackling like static. One of the vampires caught Marcus on the shoulder. He immediately used the dagger in his wrist sheath to turn his attacker to dust. A battle cry rang through the corridor. One of the vampires broke through the line, leaping down from the ceiling, snarling at me. I kicked high, catching him off guard. London's knife caught him even more off guard. Dust billowed briefly.

"We are so grounded when Mom and Dad find out about this."

"They aren't Araksaka," London said. "This isn't the royal guard."

"How do you know?"

"No tattoos."

"Bounty hunters then," Duncan said with a grunt, catching a fist to the eye. "Ow, damn it."

"No hard feelings." The female attacker grinned, jumping nimbly out of range of his return blow and kicking out at the same time. "But you're going to make us a fortune."

"Bite me, you vulture." Quinn sprawled on the tiles, groaning.

An older man in a pinstripe suit grabbed Quinn's ponytail, yanking him up.

"Hey!" I yelled, leapfrogging Duncan and the girl and elbowing another vampire, who reared up at my passing. "Get off my brother!" I wasn't fast enough or strong enough, not like they were, but I was angry and scared and they'd underestimated me. I broke Quinn's attacker's kneecap and staked him before the others could react. Quinn jumped to his feet, grinning.

"Thanks, little sister."

I grinned back, wiping my hands clean.

"Duck!" he added.

I ducked.

Vampire dust drifted over me like pollen. I sneezed.

One of the vampires, newly turned by the look of him, smiled at me as if we were on a date. "Fancy a shag?" He sniffed the air and licked his lips. "Come on, love." He sauntered over, or would have if he hadn't tripped over Logan's foot.

"Might I suggest you get the hell out of here?" Logan said, yanking on my arm. "Run, you bloody lunatic."

I ran a few steps, stopped when no one followed me. "I'm not leaving you guys here!"

"Just go!"

"No!"

"Solange!" All five of my brothers hollered my name.

"No!" I hollered back. "Come *on!*" I knew it didn't sit well with them not to finish off the last two vampires, and Mom certainly wouldn't approve either. But I just didn't want any more deaths on my hands. In the movies when a vampire dies, there's a puff of dust and everyone cheers because the bad guy's dead. In my world, the vampire might well be one of my brothers. And technically, though the bounty hunters did want me dead, I wasn't sure if they were the bad guys yet. I mean, they were following orders, right? Did they even know that I didn't want anything to do with Lady Natasha or her stupid crown? There were rules to this sort of thing, even if nobody else wanted to play by them. I also had no qualms about using guilt to my advantage.

"Who knows how many others might be out there? You want me to go alone?"

They made a collective chorus of annoyed grunts, knowing full well what I was doing, but they reluctantly came with me, which was all I'd wanted. We tore down the hall, skidding slightly on the tiles. My breath was ragged and hot in my lungs, tearing at my throat. Connor scooped me up over his shoulder, barely pausing to adjust my flailing limbs, and kept running. He was so quick, as were the rest of them, that they seemed more like washes of color around me. My stomach bounced painfully on Connor's shoulder, but we didn't stop until we'd reached a rusty door. It swung open to the moonlight trickling between the trees down onto the forest floor. Connor tossed me to my feet. I rubbed my bruised stomach.

Quinn eased ahead, peering into the undergrowth. Ferns waved their green fingers all around us. We moved quietly behind him. I might not have vampire speed or scent-tracking, but I did have Drake training and I knew how to move without being heard or seen. And I knew the forest as well as anyone, certainly better than

Logan, who preferred the city streets to mud on his expensive boots. The heady scent of pine needles and earth was soothing, cooling my throat. There wasn't a single bird or rabbit or deer. They all knew the smell of a predator, animal or otherwise. The wind tickled the oak trees. Quinn halted, held up a hand. I strained to hear what he was hearing, but all I could make out were ordinary forest sounds: the wind, the river, an owl.

"We're not alone," Logan mouthed to me.

I froze, trying not to breathe, hoping my heart wasn't pulsing like a beacon in the center of the dark woods. I might know how to step so I didn't snap twigs or crush acorns underfoot, but silencing my heartbeat was a trick I wasn't all that keen on learning. We could be as silent as we wanted, but if the vampires were near enough, they'd hear me. Frustration hummed through me. Something rustled, like bat wings.

"Get down," Logan snapped, but I was already hitting the ground. It was so dark and the vampires were so fast, it was as if shadows had collided around me, hissing. Bones shattered and mended; blood sprinkled like rain. Someone grunted. I couldn't see very well—not only was it dark, but I was half sprawled in a thicket of ferns. I scrambled up into a crouch. Logan hurtled past, cursing. The moon silvered the gleam of fangs and eyes. Another vampire rolled past me, landed on his feet.

"I smell her." He looked nearly drunk. "She's here. She's mine."

"Oh, I don't think so," I muttered grimly, reaching for a branch and breaking off the end so it was sharp and splintered. I hadn't been raised to sit around wringing my hands. We'd all known this was coming, even if I was only now truly realizing the scope and magnitude of my bloodchange. Everyone basically thought of me as a vampire broodmare, meant to give birth to lots of little royal vampire babies.

No amount of red roses sent to my door was going to make that okay.

I slammed my heel into the back of his knee as he whirled to attack Marcus. He stumbled, turned. His angry hiss shifted into a grin.

"Solange." He took a step forward. "I'm Pierre."

I lifted the branch threateningly. "Look, this is just a pheromone thing. Get over it already."

"You're even more beautiful than I thought you'd be."

"Great." The sarcasm in my voice didn't appear to register. "You know, it's been a really long night. Could you be creepy later?"

"I love you."

"Apparently not." I was feeling tired. Incredibly, I felt like yawning, even as someone grunted in pain.

"Incoming!" Quinn yelled. "There are more of them than we thought."

I tilted my head at Pierre, tried a winsome smile. Marcus stared at me.

"Are you going to be sick?"

Brothers.

"Pierre," I said. Would fluttering my eyelashes be overkill? And did I even know how to flutter my eyelashes? "Could you help me?"

"Anything for you, my love." Okay, so maybe this pheromone thing might be useful after all.

"There are bounty hunters coming." I tried to look innocent. Lucy would have fallen over laughing if she could see me now. "They want to kill me and my brothers."

"I will not let that happen," he promised fervently.

"Great." I patted his shoulder. "Go on."

He made a very dramatic departure while Marcus and I watched. Quinn and Logan joined us.

"What's going on?"

"Solange just got some sappy vamp to fight for us."

"Then what are we standing around for?" Connor said. "Let's get the hell out of here."

We ran, leaving behind the sounds of Pierre and his friends battling the bounty hunters. I really hoped he'd win. I didn't like the thought that I might have sent him to his death.

"Slowing down's not exactly the goal here," Logan said.

"Shouldn't we help him?"

"No, run faster."

"But . . ."

"Solange, you're so pale you practically glow. Move it."

I might have argued further but I was feeling very sluggish. I was barely able to push one foot in front of the other, never mind performing heroics to save a vampire who I was probably going to have to stake anyway, if the pheromones had anything to say about it.

"I feel . . . funny."

Connor scooped me up again. I was too exhausted to feel

particularly alarmed, though some part of my brain registered that this was hardly the time for a nap.

"It's just the change," he said. "You're overtired. It's normal."

The yawn was so big it made my eyes water.

"Are you sure?"

I wasn't awake long enough to hear his reassurance.

CHAPTER 14

•

Lucy

"What the bloody hell do you mean Solange went to see Veronique? And Natasha?" Everyone took a healthy step back out of range of Helena's fury. "I specifically said she wasn't to leave the house."

Liam sat in his chair and grimly drank a brandy. Hyacinth's pug was sniffing under the front door and whining. I shifted from foot to foot. The thick miasma of anger and pheromones was starting to make even me light-headed. Liam reached out for his wife's hand.

"They'll be all right," he said darkly. I'd never heard his voice have that particular tone and kind of hoped I'd never hear it again. It made the hairs on the back of my neck shiver.

"Why'd Lady Natasha set a bounty in the first place?" Nicholas asked hotly.

"There's a rumor going around," Sebastian explained. "That Solange really is going to take Lady Natasha's crown as soon as she changes."

We stared at him, all sorts of horrible scenarios unfolding in the spaces between us.

"But Solange would *hate* that," I said.

"But Lady Natasha would never want to be anything else," Helena said. "So she'll never understand that, or trust it. Also, she knows Montmartre is courting Solange, in his own twisted fashion. Even though they haven't been together for a long time, she doesn't share well." She glanced at the window. "Where the bloody hell is Hyacinth? It'll be dawn soon."

"Bruno has his boys out looking for her."

"I should be with them." Sebastian was standing stiffly in the corner, glowering.

"No." Helena narrowed her eyes in his direction.

"Mom."

"I said no, Sebastian. You've done enough tonight."

"What about London?" Nicholas asked. "She's the one who came to get Solange."

Liam sighed. "She's a royalist, like the rest of that side of the family. But I have to believe she didn't know about the danger."

"There's more." Geoffrey tapped his pen on the cover of a leather-bound book. His hair stuck up everywhere; he'd been raking his hand through it constantly since he got here. Liam tilted his head back and briefly closed his eyes.

"Of course there is."

"I've finished analyzing the Hypnos sample."

Liam straightened, his eyes flaring like hot silver.

"Tell me."

"Several zombie drugs, as we'd assumed," Geoffrey said.

"And?"

His expression was hard. He didn't look like a slightly distracted scientist anymore, or like the handsome intellectual who attracted all the divorced women in town.

"It's ancient blood. Ancient enough to be Enheduanna."

The silence fell like a hammer through a glass window. I blinked.

"Who's Enheduanna?" I whispered to Nicholas. No one was speaking. It was kind of creepy, actually. "Hello?"

"An ancient." Geoffrey was the one to answer me, though he didn't glance my way. The fire crackled softly, falling to embers in the grate. "The oldest vampire still alive."

"Oh. Um, and?"

"And her blood has magical effects. Like Hypnos, it takes away your will."

"I remember." I stifled a shiver.

"On vampires too, not just on humans."

"Oh." My eyes widened. "Oh!"

"Indeed," Geoffrey agreed drily. "And now it's in the hands of the Helios-Ra."

"Who are only marginally better than Lady Natasha or her tribes." Helena's black braid lifted into the air as she whirled to kick the leg of a spindly Queen Anne chair. It splintered loudly.

"That was my mother's," Liam murmured.

"This is bad," Nicholas said to me. "The thing about vampires, of any kind, is that we're supposedly immune to each other's pheromones. It's what's stopped us from wiping each other out entirely with clan wars."

"But not anymore," I whispered.

"Not anymore."

"How did they even get it?" Sebastian asked.

"I can assure you I plan on asking Hart that myself," Liam said through his teeth. "He's on his way here."

"Here?" Sebastian gaped at him. "You're not serious."

"He was amenable."

"Amenable to staking each and every one of us in our own home," Sebastian muttered.

"No, we're safest here and we outnumber him. I allowed him only a single companion."

"And a bucket of Hypnos powder."

"Sebastian," Helena snapped. "Your father knows what he's doing."

Liam smiled.

"I'll remind you of that, love."

Nicholas sat down, shaking his head.

"So, the head of the Helios-Ra is coming here for tea, they have Hypnos at their disposal, Solange is possibly in the hands of the vampire queen who set the bounty on her head, and we can't find Aunt Hyacinth. That about cover it?" He looked suddenly young and overwhelmed, like the Nicholas I'd known before he turned. I touched his shoulder. Before I could think of a single helpful thing to say, Liam's cell phone vibrated in his jacket pocket. He glanced at the display.

"Bruno." He and Helena exchanged a grim look. "Hart's here, and Hope." They looked at us.

"Lucy and Nicholas, upstairs."

"Mom!"

"But—"

"Now," Liam insisted. "Lucy, the presence of a human girl will not help our cause at the moment. And Nicholas, you can barely stand."

He was rather wobbly on his feet. Dawn must be filling the garden on the other side of the drapes. We shuffled upstairs, reluctant but obedient.

More or less.

Mom says my temper isn't my only karmic baggage. I have this thing about taking orders, no matter how well meant. And though I completely understood why it might be best to remain out of sight, it hardly followed that I should sit alone in Solange's room and not know what was going on. Just because they shouldn't see me didn't mean I shouldn't see them.

"Lucy?" Nicholas whispered, stopping when he realized I wasn't following. "What are you doing?"

In point of fact I was lying on my stomach at the top of the curving staircase. From this vantage I could see the front door. I couldn't see into the living room, but I heard Helena ask Sebastian if he wanted to retire and his emphatic refusal. He was newly turned—it had only been a few years, after all—but I wouldn't have left either if I were him. No matter how exhausted I was.

Lucy

I wondered again where Solange was. And if she was okay.

"They can hear your heartbeat, you know." Nicholas stretched out next to me.

"Hey, I'm upstairs. Technically I'm not breaking the rules." I slid him a sidelong glance. "Can they really hear my exact location?"

"Probably not," he admitted. He was very close. I could feel the cool length of his body pressing against mine. His eyes were very pale, his teeth very sharp. If I was immune to his pheromones, then why did I find him so annoyingly attractive?

A knock sounded at the front door. The dogs barreled into the foyer, growling. Mrs. Brown barked from behind Hyacinth's bedroom door. Bruno escorted the heads of Helios-Ra inside, his expression implacable and hard. He considered the Drakes his own family, and Solange an honorary niece.

"Hart and Hope," I muttered. "If you're going to name your kids like that, of course they're going to think they live in a comic book." Although I had to admit Hart was handsome, practically debonair. His hair was threaded with silver and rakishly messy. "Okay, he's totally got that yummy secret agent thing going on."

Nicholas scowled at me. I didn't have to turn my head to look at him to feel his eyes burning.

Hope was short, barely five feet tall, with a cheerful face and a ponytail swinging from the crown of her head. She wore jeans and a thick leather belt hung with stakes under her long sweater, and sandals. Somehow I hadn't expected her to be so perky, in her strappy silver sandals.

"They're going in," I whispered.

"I can see that," Nicholas muttered. His nose twitched.

"You look like a demented bunny," I told him. "What are you doing?"

"You switched to lemon shampoo."

I blinked, thought back to my morning shower, which felt like years ago. He was right. His hands were clenched, but his voice was soft and husky. He turned his head away, was close enough that his hair brushed my cheek.

"Smells good."

CHAPTER 15

◆

Solange

I only woke up because I had a mouthful of mud and a lump of hard dirt as a pillow.

"Ow." I sat up, blinking blearily. "What the hell, you guys?"

"Shh," Connor hissed at me, his hand covering my mouth. "We're not alone." I could barely hear him, he was speaking so softly. I couldn't hear heartbeats or frightened porcupines or twigs snapping under combat boots, but I knew the rest of my brothers could. He drew a sun in the dirt at our feet. I could barely make out the shape in the moonlight falling through the branches. Not just vampires then.

Helios-Ra.

The wind was warm, persistent. The crickets had stopped singing, no doubt sensing predators in every corner of the forest. This was our forest, damn it. The Helios-Ra had no business here.

Shadows flitted between the trees, making an unearthly sigh of displaced air. A vampire screamed and turned to dust, billowing between the leaves. A wooden Helios-Ra stake bit the maple tree behind her as she crumbled. Someone screeched. Connor leaped into the fray before I could stop him. Marcus was fighting, and Quinn, of course, who couldn't be kept from a good fight no matter the circumstances. Logan crouched between me and the worst of it, Duncan was farther behind, guarding our back. It was standard formation, one my mother drilled into us along with our ABCs and why we mustn't tell anyone our parents had fangs and drank blood instead of coffee. For my mother to have been truly proud, we should have had the high ground.

We didn't.

In fact, we weren't even all accounted for. "Where's London?" I asked.

"She took off," Logan answered grimly. "She ran off down some tunnel while you were napping."

"And you didn't go after her?"

"Little busy for a temper tantrum."

"She probably feels bad about dragging me to court."

"Too busy for that, too. She'll be fine," he added. "And anyway, she mentioned something about doing some recon of her own. The royal guard should have been there to protect you if you were such an honored guest. She wants to know what's going on."

"Everything's a sad-ass mess, is what's going on," I muttered. "Doesn't take a genius to figure that out."

I didn't even know how far away from the farm we were, having slept through a good part of the journey. We could be half an hour away or three hours. The stars were faint above us, visible only when there was a particularly violent gust of wind. I studied their patterns, as much as I was able. The moon hung low.

"Nearly dawn," I muttered at Logan. "We have to get out of here."

"You think?" he muttered back, using that tone reserved for only the most annoying of little sisters. I rose to my feet, feeling as if I were moving through water. I was that tired, with my eyes burning and my throat clenched against a yawn. Logan glared at me.

"Get back down."

I shook my head. "We're outnumbered."

"Not the first time," he grunted, ramming a stake into the heart of a vampire Connor flipped toward him. A hiss, a burst of dust.

"I can smell her," someone interrupted, excitement thrumming through his voice. I had no desire whatsoever to meet the owner of that voice. The moon continued to drop behind the horizon. I dove toward Logan, coming up at his side. I yanked stakes out of his back holster.

"Stay down, damn it."

"She's mine." One of the vampires caught my scent and turned sharply away from where he'd been beating Duncan to a pulp. The vampire looked around, distracted. "Solange? I'm here for you, my love."

"If he starts spouting poetry I'm staking him myself," I promised through my teeth. Duncan rolled toward us, a deep gash bleeding profusely on his head. Blood matted his hair to the side of his face. Logan's nostrils flared.

"Cutting it close, aren't you?" he muttered.

"Bastard's stronger than he looks," Duncan muttered back as I propped him up against a tree. I swallowed against the gag reflex when his blood oozed over my fingers.

"Are you okay?"

"I'm fine." He wiped his face with his sleeve. "It's healing already."

The sounds of battle came closer.

Too close.

I heard the snap of a twig. And then Marcus roaring. Not a twig. His arm.

I threw one of my stakes. It didn't hit the vampire's heart but she did stumble back, hissing. Marcus hid himself in the bushes, cradling his injured arm. Quinn laughed even though he was fighting off a vampire and a Helios-Ra agent who were also fighting each other. Fists thudded into flesh. Blood splattered through the air. The darkness was fading slowly to the gray light of predawn, glinting off night-vision equipment. I sat back on my heels, stomach clenching.

"Logan," I said. "There's too many of them."

"We're fine," he insisted.

"Are not," I insisted right back. "You guys have to get out of here."

"We're trying," Duncan grunted.

"I mean right now. Without me."

"Forget it."

"We have you surrounded," a voice announced over some kind of scratchy amplifier. Quinn blinked, midpunch.

"Cops?"

"Worse," the vampire currently ducking hissed. "Helios-Ra."

"Damn it all to hell, they're not even being subtle about it."

"We only want the girl, not the bounty," the amplified voice shouted out. "We're willing to let the rest of you go."

"Bite me," Quinn suggested.

"And me," his new friend agreed.

The sun was hovering on the edge of the horizon. I could see it in my brothers' faces. A fine sweat beaded Logan's forehead, and vampire body temperature was generally much lower than human temperature. To see one sweat was rare. Very rare. His face looked drawn too, nearly gray with fatigue. Duncan's hand shook as he shoved himself to his feet.

We could probably fight our way through the others. After all, they'd have to seek cover soon, just as we would. But even if we did get through them with minor damage, we still had to get through the Helios-Ra, who could lie out in the bright sunlight and just wait for my brothers to sicken and die. My choices were narrowing drastically. I knew what I had to do. I also knew that each and every one of my pig-headed brothers was faster than me. I couldn't hope to outrun them.

But I could take them by surprise.

I let them mutter among themselves, let Logan pull me to my feet. The other vampires scattered, like earwigs under a shifted stone. The leaves barely trembled at their passing. Quinn and Marcus closed in and Connor moved toward us through the undergrowth. An arrow whistled between the trees and hit him in the shoulder. He jerked back, clutching at his bloody arm.

"I'm all right," he told us, jaw clenched in pain.

"A warning shot," an agent called out. "Next time we hit the heart."

My brothers were scowling at each other, dragging Connor to safety.

Now or never.

If I thought about it too long I might wimp out.

Now.

I eased away from Duncan, who was half-turned away to prop up Connor. Only Logan blocked me and he wasn't expecting me to knee him in the kidney and then leapfrog over him as he doubled over.

So that was exactly what I did.

A rain of Helios-Ra arrows flew over me, biting the ground behind me like the ramparts of a castle fort. They protected me from my brothers, who had to halt their forward charge, if only for a moment.

"Your word," I yelled, running even though my legs felt like lead and my lungs burned. "Your word my brothers go free."

"Take her."

They swarmed around me like beetles. I jerked away, all instinct and thrumming adrenaline. They were faceless, eye goggles obscuring their features, and black vests, black pants, black boots.

The sun crested the horizon, dripping softly between the leaves.

"Run, you idiots!" I hollered at my brothers as my arms were seized. I knew they didn't really have any other option. The sun was now bleeding through the trees. They wouldn't even be able to make it home. They'd have to use one of the caves or the secret safe houses, and by house, I really meant hole in the ground.

"Got her."

"This is her?" one of the agents said as they began to march me through the forest. A few of his companions were hobbling, one was being carried. "She's just a kid."

I knew what he saw: a fifteen-year-old girl in a muddy slip dress and scratches all over her arms from running through the woods. His companion shrugged.

"Bounty's the same. And anyway, come her birthday she'll be a monster like the rest of them."

"The Drakes are all right," someone else muttered. "They're on the Raktapa Council, at least. Now, would you stop your damn gossip and hurry the hell up?"

I was so tired I could barely see straight. I shuffled my feet, hardly having the energy to lift them off the ground.

"What's the matter with you?" he snapped. "Are you hurt?"

"I'm *tired*."

"Fresh out of coffee, princess, so move your ass."

The morning continued to unfurl around us in pink misty dampness, as if we sat in the center of a rose after a rain. The leaves shivered above us, so green they nearly glowed. Birds sang cheerfully, oblivious to my predicament. Pine needles crunched under our passage.

"Where are you taking me?" I asked, biting back a yawn.

They didn't answer as they formed a tight circle around me, one I knew I had no hope of breaking through, especially since I felt about as strong as a wet noodle. I squinted at the sunlight, eyes tearing. I hoped my brothers were safe. They'd be nearly defense-less. Each of them was still new enough to the bloodchange that they slept hard, too hard to defend themselves quickly if there was an attack.

We continued to march along until I began to recognize where we were. The mountains were on our right and a small lake glis-tened in a lower valley. The tunnel ran right underneath us, no one the wiser. I was so close to an escape and it might as well have been on the other side of the planet for all the good it did me. Even if I could get to one of the doorways, which was doubtful, I couldn't afford to give away the secret location to the Helios-Ra. I was thinking so hard I didn't see the shadow leap down from a tall gray aspen, scowling fiercely. He wore unrelieved black like the others and was armed to the teeth. His dark eyes pinned me.

"What the hell is she doing here?"

Kieran Black.

CHAPTER 16

•

Lucy

Saturday night, very late

I ignored the pleasantries being stiffly exchanged since Nicholas was lying really close to me. It was so wrong that I wanted to snuggle against his side.

It was *Nicholas.*

Byron was a welcome distraction as he ambled up the stairs and lay on my other side. He had kibble breath and was close enough that he drooled on my arm. I nudged him.

"Move over, you big lump." He just gave me that doggy look, the pathetic one I could never resist. "Fine, but at least quit drooling on me. It's gross." I scratched his ear briefly. "Some watchdog you are." I knew the other two Bouviers would be lying down near Hart and Hope, eyeing them hungrily.

"I want to assure you," Hart was saying in the living room, "that I have officially retracted the bounty on the Drake clan, just so there are no more misunderstandings."

"We're glad to hear it," Liam said blandly. I could just imagine what retort Helena was biting back.

"It was an accident," Hart continued, sounding hard. "And one that will be rectified immediately."

"I suggest you keep a closer rein on your organization," Helena said. "Or I will cease to keep such a tight rein on mine."

"Understood. We stand by our treaty," Hope interjected. "This is an internal problem and should never have leaked out."

Their voices dropped slightly. There was the clink of glasses. I squirmed, trying to peer around the stairs into the living room. I could see the edge of a chair and nothing else. There wasn't even anyone sitting in it.

"I'm going to try and get closer," I murmured.

When Nicholas didn't try and stop me, I turned to look at him. He was asleep. His cheek rested on his hand, pale skin gleaming, dark brown hair tousled. His features were sculpted, sensual, and dark. It was totally unfair how beautiful he was. Even if it did sound like he might be snoring a little. Byron snorted and rolled over.

"You two are a lot of help," I said.

And then the quiet shattered.

There was no actual sound of warning, only Hart sailing out of the living room, crashing into the foyer wall and sprawling across the floor in a heap. The chandelier above him rattled alarmingly. At the sound, Nicholas startled awake and flipped himself over me, as if he was protecting me from an airborne missile. He pressed into me, about as yielding as a slab of cold marble. He looked slightly disoriented, not quite fully awake.

"Can't breathe," I croaked.

He shifted slightly but didn't get off me. I could see the thick fringe of his eyelashes, his hair falling over his forehead to tickle mine.

"Foyer," I wheezed. We both craned our necks. Helena marched out, all black leather and motherly fury. Byron raced down the stairs.

"Where is my daughter?" She seethed, her pale eyes practically glowing. Liam flanked her, simmering. I could all but see the leash on his temper straining to release. Hope took a stake from her belt.

"I wouldn't," Bruno advised quietly.

"What the hell was that for?" Hart sat up, his left eye already purpling.

Liam lifted his cell phone. "That was one of my sons, gone to ground because of your blasted league."

"I told you we didn't set the damn bounty," Hart said through his teeth. "I explained."

"Then explain to me, human," Helena sneered, "why my daughter has been taken by your agents."

Hart stared at her. "What?"

Sebastian and Geoffrey joined them from the living room. Boudicca barked once, blocking Hart from doing anything more than sitting up. Nicholas shifted off me, growling low in his throat.

"That's impossible," Hart insisted. He reached for his own cell phone and punched in a number. He barked out questions, swore viciously under his breath at the replies. Sunlight touched the windows on either side of the door.

"Unit's gone rogue," he declared.

Hope paled. "No."

Helena sniffed the air delicately, then nodded at her husband. "He's not lying."

Beside me, Nicholas sniffed as well. He frowned. I frowned back.

"What?"

"It's not a lie, but I smell something else. Something I can't quite place."

"More lemon shampoo?"

"No. Definitely not that."

Bruno signaled to the dogs and they eased back, letting Hart get to his feet.

"We have to shut them down," he said darkly. I wondered if he had a gun strapped inside a shoulder holster under his coat. "Now. Before the damage becomes irrevocable."

"I am forced to agree." Liam held up a hand. "However, we had a treaty, Hart. And it was broken. Under the circumstances, I believe a show of faith is in order."

Hart sighed. "What did you have in mind, Drake?"

"One of you stays here."

"You're taking hostages now?"

"You have our daughter. Her safety must be assured."

"You have our word," Hope said.

Liam raised one eyebrow. "Not nearly good enough."

Hart rubbed his face wearily. "All right. All right," he repeated. "I'll stay."

Hope whirled on him. "No, I'll stay. You know how some of the units still see me as a paper pusher. They'll respond to you quicker and with less posturing if they truly have gone rogue." She squared her shoulders. "So, I'll stay." She narrowed her eyes. "You don't have a dungeon, do you? Because I expect a guest room." She showed her teeth in a bare approximation of a smile. "As a show of good faith, of course."

Hart met Liam's grim gaze, returned it with his own. "I expect her to be safe here."

Liam inclined his head. "As long as our daughter is safe."

Hart barely suppressed a wince. "I'll do my best," he said.

"If your best isn't good enough?" Helena said softly, silkily. "I will personally drain every single person in your league. Understood?"

He nodded stiffly.

"Your mom rocks," I muttered. "You know he's totally shaking under all that suave sophistication."

Bruno showed Hart outside, trailed by the dogs, except for Byron, who kept sniffing suspiciously at Hope. Geoffrey nodded his head at the stairs.

"Your room is this way."

Nicholas and I scrambled to our feet. He pulled me down the hall, his fingers like a vise around mine. We leaped into Solange's room just as Geoffrey led Hope to one of the guest rooms with its own bathroom. He shut the door behind her and locked it, with an ominous click that seemed to reverberate. He paused on the other side of Solange's door, and I half expected him to lock us in as well.

"Get to sleep, you two," he muttered before walking away.

I turned back to Nicholas, who was already stretched out on Solange's bed, his head resting on the Hello Kitty pillow I'd given her for her ninth birthday.

"What do we do now?" I asked. My eyes felt gritty and dry. I'd been awake for nearly twenty-four hours. I felt a little lightheaded. Nicholas didn't even open his eyes.

"I have to sleep." His words were slurred. I sat down next to him, touched his forehead. There was an unhealthy pallor to his skin. "Save Solange."

He didn't say anything else for a long time. I poked him once. "Nicholas?"

Nothing.

It felt wrong to sleep when my best friend was out there at the mercy of rogue vampire hunters. Buffy wouldn't have slept.

Of course, Buffy had supernatural powers.

Me?

Not so much.

"Shut up about Buffy already," Nicholas muttered. I hadn't even realized I'd spoken out loud. He didn't open his eyes, only reached out and yanked my sleeve until I fell over, sprawled next to him. "Go to sleep."

The bed was soft and smelled like vanilla fabric softener. Nicholas was a comforting presence against me. He was already asleep again. He wouldn't notice if I snuggled in just a little bit closer.

For safety's sake, of course. There were bad guys everywhere, after all. One couldn't be too careful.

He shifted midsnore and pulled me closer.

I fell asleep feeling better than I had all week.

CHAPTER 17

◆

Solange

"Get lost, Black, this doesn't concern you." The agent in the lead tensed. His shoulders knotted and his hand strayed to the hilt of his weapon. Sunlight glinted off his night-vision goggles, pushed up on his head. The others exchanged wary glances. There was something in the air, some secret I didn't know about.

"Like hell it doesn't," Kieran said.

"Look, we don't need you, kid. Go home."

"Go to hell," Kieran shot back. "I'm a full agent and deserve a cut."

Whatever was sizzling around us seemed to relax slightly.

"What are you saying, Black?"

"I'm saying the bounty's enough for all of us."

Someone snorted. "Your uncle know you're doing this? Or haven't you heard? Helios called us off."

"What?" I asked. "Then what the hell are you doing with me?"

Kieran ignored me. Black nose plugs hung around his neck and stakes lined the leather strap across his chest.

"Vampire queen's still got a bounty on her, doesn't she? I want in," he repeated.

I hadn't known that, either. I was starting to hate my sixteenth birthday. A poufy white dress and a cake with roses made out of pink icing and awkward dancing with boys in awkward suits was starting to sound like a great alternative. Seriously. Sign me up. I wouldn't even complain.

"You'll have to prove yourself."

Kieran shoved up his sleeve, showing his sun tattoo. "I've proven myself, thanks."

"We're taking out more than one little girl, no matter how freaky she might be."

"Whatever, look, I just want the money." He pushed toward me. The woods seemed to glow so brightly, I shaded my face. My vision was more sensitive than it had ever been. The trees might as well have been carved out of emeralds and filled with sunlight. His eyes were soothingly dark.

And glaring at me pointedly.

I glared back.

He broke contact only long enough to glance to his right, brief as a lightning bug's flash. My glare lost some of its oomph as I tried to figure out what was going on. The agents were spread out slightly on his right. Not enough to make an escape, but almost. Kieran tripped over a tree root, his elbow catching one of the guards in the sternum. He stumbled back. The gap widened. Kieran grabbed my hand and tossed me through the brief opening. I could feel him at my back, pushing me on. Behind us the agents hollered. A shot rang out, pinged bark off a pine tree not a foot from my head. Kieran shoved me. "Run faster."

"Trying," I gasped. Only adrenaline kept me going, and it was starting to make me feel sick. There was nothing quiet or vampiric about the way I was crashing through the woods. A deaf and blind kitten could have followed my trail.

They were closing in.

We'd never be able to outrun them. Especially not since I was already wheezing and stumbling. I tripped over my own foot and went sprawling in the dirt. Kieran reached down to haul me back up.

"Wait, don't," I said. I recognized the nick in the oak near my head, right near the root. At first glance it wouldn't have been noticeable, at second it would have looked like a deer or a coyote had rubbed up against it. But I knew what it was.

Safety notch.

And sure enough, when I clawed through the undergrowth, I found the wooden handle, carved to look like an exposed root covered in moss. The actual door was just a chunk of wood and it was painstakingly covered with mud and leaves that camouflaged it even after it had been opened.

"Are you nuts? Get up!"

Instead I pushed into a crouch and yanked at the handle. It opened to a deep hole with a rope secured to the side and dangling down to the bottom.

"Let's go," I told him, sliding in feetfirst. The rope burned my

hands. Kieran followed, the door shutting with a thunk above our heads. Darkness swallowed us as my feet hit the ground. Kieran landed beside me. I reached out tentatively to run my hand over the walls, feeling dirt and roots as thin as hair. The dirt gave way to Kieran's shoulder.

"Um . . . sorry."

I could hear his ragged breathing, and my own breath burned in my lungs. There wasn't much space to maneuver. I shifted away, hit the wall behind me. Shifted again and my hip bumped his. His hand closed over my arm.

"Wait." His voice was husky. I heard him rummaging. I wondered if I should be worried about Hypnos powder. But it didn't make sense for him to drug me after he'd helped me get away.

Unless he wanted the bounty for himself.

I was close enough that I should be able to hit some vital organ with my foot or my fist. If he was unconscious while I was under the effects of the Hypnos, he couldn't take advantage of my hypnotized state. There was a click and I launched myself at him. His arms closed around me, and we hit the wall with enough force to rattle my insides. My teeth cut into the inside of my lip. I tasted blood.

A blue glow from the lightstick he'd broken filled the cramped space.

He hadn't been reaching for Hypnos after all—he'd only been trying to find us a light source in his belt.

"What the hell?" He grunted, rubbing his bruised knee. I was pressed against him, chest to ankle. I struggled, leaning back. I didn't have any strength left. My angry leap had sapped the very last of it. I sagged a little.

"I thought you were going for the Hypnos powder."

His eyes were very dark in the weird blue light. His eyebrows nearly snapped together, he was glowering so deeply.

"I've been *trying* to save your life."

"Um. Thanks?" I tried a smile, then decided on just glowering back. "Look, it was an honest mistake."

"If you say so."

He still hadn't let go of me. When he released his hold, I leaned against the wall, closing my eyes.

"What's the matter with you?" he asked. I could hear the concern in his voice, under all that irritation. "Are you hurt?"

"Bloodchange."

"What . . . right now?" He might have just possibly squeaked.

"In about two days, actually. Happy birthday to me."

"Isn't it supposed to make you get stronger?"

"Sure," I said drily. "If it doesn't kill me first."

"We can't stay here."

"The tunnel leads to another safe room."

"They won't stop searching for us. They'll comb the whole forest."

"I can't run anymore," I said apologetically. "I just can't. Pull that lever there, by your head."

He pulled it down and then leaped back out of the way when a gate swung closed, blocking access to the tunnel.

"This way," I told him, literally dragging my feet. He came up beside me, putting his arm around my waist to help me. "I'm okay," I muttered.

"You're practically green. Except for the lovely bloodshot eyes, of course."

"Oh." My vanity twinged. I knew it was stupid; I had way bigger problems. But I still didn't want to look like a haggard, disgusting mess around him. He was warm against me, and I felt chilled and was trembling with it suddenly. The damp of being underground didn't help. My teeth chattered. I just needed to get to a corner where I could collapse. Kieran half carried me down the passageway. It smelled like mud and green and water, dripping somewhere we couldn't see. The tunnel widened and then we were in a round chamber with flagstones on the ground and a narrow bed in the back corner. There was a chest I knew was filled with blankets, matches, and various other supplies, including a thermos of blood. There was another gate, locked with an alarm system. The red light blinked like an eye. Kieran helped me to the bed, then stared at the alarm as I leaned over to pull blankets out of the metal chest.

"Can you get that open?"

I shook my head. "The grate you closed in the tunnel and that door there are both automatically wired to stay locked until sunset." I raised an eyebrow. "I'm sure I don't have to explain why."

"I had no idea any of this was down here. It's like an old-time war bunker."

"It's been here for at least a hundred years. It helps us get around and stay out of the sun." I leaned back on the blankets, yawning. "And since we're constantly being attacked by snipers and warriors and idiots, I guess it kind of is like war."

"Am I a sniper, a warrior, or an idiot?"

"Don't know yet."

"Well, thanks very much for that." He frowned, glancing around. "If the Helios-Ra find the opening, we'll be trapped in here."

"They won't find it—it's really well camouflaged. And there are ways around the alarm if we really need them. But we don't yet." I tried to call my parents but my cell phone wouldn't work. "Low battery," I muttered. "Figures." I looked at him. "What about your phone?"

"If I turn it on now, Helios will activate the GPS chip." His voice softened. "So I guess we just wait."

My eyelids were so heavy. I had to assume I could trust him not to stake me if I fell asleep, because I wasn't going to be able *not* to fall asleep for much longer. And he'd proven himself trustworthy enough for a nap. I heard him rummaging in the chest and then the scratch and hiss of a match being lit and the wick of a fat candle catching. The artificial blue glow faded to candlelight. The smell of melting wax crowded out the damp.

"Are you scared, Solange?"

My eyes popped open briefly. He was watching me carefully, seated on a folded blanket on top of the chest. The flickering light glinted off the edge of the goggles loose around his neck and the snaps on his cargo pants and the metal under the scraped leather of his combat boots.

"Scared of what?"

"Being a vampire."

I glanced away, glanced back. He was still looking at me, as if there was nothing else worth contemplating in the world.

"Sometimes," I whispered truthfully. "Not so much about being a vampire—that's all I've ever known. More about the change." I shivered. "The last of my brothers to go through it nearly didn't come out the other side."

"I didn't think it was that dangerous."

"It's why they confused it with consumption in the nineteenth century."

"Consumption?"

"Tuberculosis."

"Oh." He paused. "Really?"

"They don't teach you this at the academy?" I couldn't help a very small sneer.

He didn't sneer back. "No."

Now I felt bad for being petty. He had saved my life, after all.

"We have the same symptoms as tuberculosis, especially in the eyes of the Romantic Poets. Pale, tired, coughing up blood."

"That's romantic?"

I had to smile. "Romantic with a capital 'R.' You know, like Byron and Coleridge."

He gave a mock shudder. "Please, stop. I barely passed English Lit."

I snorted. "I didn't have that option. One of my aunts took Byron as a lover."

"Get out."

"Seriously. It makes Lucy insanely jealous."

"That girl is . . ."

"My best friend," I filled in sternly.

"I was only going to say she's unique."

"Okay, then." The room was spinning slowly, the edges blurry. I wouldn't be able to fight the lethargy much longer. "Just so we're clear."

"She's just as protective of you as you are of her, you know." I could hear the smile in his voice.

"I know. I'm worried about her. I think this is going to get really ugly."

"I think you're right."

"Is it true Helios called off the bounty?"

"Yes."

I turned over onto my side so I could see him without having to hold up my head, which now weighed approximately as much as a car. "Then why are they after me?"

His posture changed, as if something that had been holding him up wasn't there any longer. "One of the units has gone rogue. I got a call before, just as they found you and your brothers."

I rested my cheek on my hands. "That really happens? Units going rogue, I mean?"

"It hasn't in nearly two hundred years, but yes, it happens. It's been a bad year for the league. My uncle's in charge, and he's great, he really is, but since his partner was replaced, it hasn't been the same."

"Why not? Who was his partner?"

"My father."

I had to ask. I didn't know what to say. I remembered him saying his father was killed by a vampire. Which made me want to apologize. Which was ridiculous. I hadn't killed him and neither had anyone I knew, so why would I apologize? Would he apologize to me for the Helios-Ra agent who'd killed one of my cousin's girl-friends?

Still. He'd lost his father.

"I'm sorry your father died."

His jaw clenched. "Thank you." His voice was very husky.

"We didn't do it."

Something bloomed right then and there in the small dark space between us. I didn't know what it was, but I knew enough to know it was rare and delicate. And it felt so real I might have been able to reach out and touch it if I tried.

"You can go to sleep," he told me softly. "I'll look after you."

CHAPTER 18

•

Lucy

Sunday afternoon

I woke up late the next day, smothered by my very own vampire blanket. I shifted experimentally but Nicholas didn't budge. His arms were wrapped around me, pinning me ruthlessly to his chest. That might sound passionate in romance novels, but in real life, it was uncomfortable. My arm was asleep, my nose was mashed against his chest, and I really had to pee.

"Nicholas," I whispered.

Nothing.

I pushed his shoulder.

Still nothing.

None of those same novels had ever made any suggestions as to the extraction of one's self from a superhuman embrace. There were logistical issues. Such as the fact that I could break my own arm trying to squirm away and he'd sleep right through it. I squirmed anyway, just in case.

"Damn it, Nicky, wake up, you undead slug."

It wasn't a good sign when I couldn't even irritate him into a response. There was a narrow window beside Solange's bed. I might just be able to reach it with my toe. I stretched until the arch of my foot and the back of my calf began to cramp painfully.

"This is ridiculous," I huffed, stretching farther. I could feel my face going red with the effort. With my luck, this would be the exact moment he woke up—to find me inches from his head, straining and panting like I was passing a kidney stone.

I finally managed to hook the cord of the blinds with my toes. One yank and a quick release and the blinds snapped up. Late-afternoon sunlight slanted over the bed and across his pale, still face. The glass was treated, of course, so it wasn't dangerous, but Nicholas's young vampire instinct made him recoil from the sudden fall of light. He burrowed under the security of blankets, shifting his arm and throwing it over his head for good measure.

The only problem was that he did it so fast, the momentum shoved me right off the bed and onto the floor. I landed with a squeak and a particularly ungraceful display of flailing limbs, neither of which helped to make my landing any softer.

My elbow tingled and my tailbone throbbed, and I now had intimate knowledge of the dust bunnies under Solange's bed. And the patchwork skirt I thought I'd lost last year, twisted under a storage box covered in stickers. Yes, even little girls with vampire lineage have a sticker phase. I shoved to my feet, grimacing. Nicholas slept on peacefully, looking exactly like a marble carving of a sleep-ing angel. Hah.

There was nothing angelic about the way he kissed.

When I caught myself snickering, I realized I must be groggier than I thought. I hurried out of the room before I embarrassed myself irrevocably. The house was quiet. Boudicca lay in front of Hope's door. She wagged her tail when she saw me but otherwise didn't move. Liam must have sent her to guard the bedroom. I went to fetch Mrs. Brown and then let her out to terrorize the wildlife in the backyard. One thing I'd learned in my family was that if you had an animal companion, never "pet," who was depen-dent on you, you lived up to your responsibilities. No excuses. Ever. When I was seven I'd begged my parents for a goldfish because I loved feeding the ones at the Buddhist temple we went to every New Year's Eve. Only I forgot to feed mine, and it floated belly-up one sad Sunday morning. To say that my mother overre-acted was to vastly underestimate my mother. We had a funeral, complete with a papier-mâché Viking boat, which she set on fire, sending my goldfish's spirit to Valhalla via Lake Violet.

"Hurry up," I called over to Mrs. Brown, who was wiggling her little pug bottom in joy at finding one of Byron's abandoned beef bones on the edge of the lawn. The sun was soft, like warm honey poured onto the treetops and the roses, glittering over the win-dows of the farmhouse. It was one of those perfect long summer days just before school starts. Solange and I usually wandered around town, complaining about how bored we were and how much it sucked that I had to go back to school and she had to learn how to pour tea in the precise Victorian way. You know, in case Charlotte Brontë ever dropped by for tea cakes. I would have given anything to be that bored right now.

I wished we knew where Solange was and whether she was all right. We didn't even know if she was still conscious. There were only two days left until her birthday. If someone wasn't there to help her through her bloodchange, she'd be dead before she even got a chance to be sixteen—or else she'd turn into a *Hel-Blar*.

If she wasn't already dead.

"Can't think like that," I muttered, shredding the rose I hadn't realized I'd picked. Torn petals drifted messily to the ground. Mrs. Brown attacked them as if they offended her sense of order. I didn't hear the window slide open over her fierce growls, but I did hear Hope raise her voice.

"Lucky, isn't it?"

"No one calls me that." I looked up, shading my eyes. "There are alarms on the windows, and if you jump, Byron will chase you." I snapped my fingers at the shaggy dog, who slunk over from the porch, head lowered submissively as soon as he saw Mrs. Brown. As a threat, he needed work.

"I'm not going to jump," Hope assured me. "Anyway, I'd break my leg from this distance."

"Good." I didn't know what else to say.

"I can get you away from here," she added softly.

Now I knew exactly what to say.

"Not you, too," I said impatiently. "I'm not a prisoner, and the Drakes aren't monsters. They're family."

"You're not a vampire." Her expression darkened. I wouldn't have thought such a cheerful face could look so angry. "Did they change you?"

"No, of course not." I scowled back. "Wait, how did you know my name?"

"You're Solange's closest friend. Of course we know who you are."

"That stupid field guide, right? Do you also know how creepy you are? Stalking a fifteen-year-old girl in your commando outfits?"

"But drinking blood isn't creepy?"

"No creepier than eating a dead cow."

She shook her head. "Kieran said you wouldn't be interested in detox."

"Detox? From what? My friends?"

"From vampires. From this lifestyle." She waved a hand at the treated glass. "From alarm systems and nightwalkers and sword-fights."

"Okay, first of all, I happen to love swordfighting. And second of all, what, your lifestyle of secret agent assassins is somehow sub-urban white bread all of a sudden? Please."

"Oh, Lucky, it's not like that."

"It's Lucy," I corrected her through my teeth. "And your people tried to kill my best friend, so you'll forgive me if I'm not overly keen on learning the secret handshake."

She shook her head sadly. "You should be going on dates and hanging out at the mall. Not wearing stakes on your belt."

I shrugged one shoulder. "The mall sucks."

"I can help you."

"Like you helped Solange? No thanks."

"You can have a normal life. It's not too late for you."

I nearly laughed. "You've clearly never met my parents. Normal was never an option." I folded my arms and smiled at her sarcastically. "You could leave the Helios-Ra. We could help you stop trying to kill people just because they have a medical condition that you don't understand."

She sucked in a breath. "It's not like that."

"It's totally like that. *God.*"

"You're so young. You can't see the bigger picture."

"I'm sixteen, I'm not an idiot."

"We could use you." She made it sound like it was something I should be excited about. "There's so much we could teach you. You have the instinct for it, I can tell."

The thought made me shiver. "No."

"The offer stands. If you should change your mind." She looked young, with her ponytail and her round cheeks. Still, her eyes were old, knowing. I was spared further conversation when Bruno came striding out of the wooded area bordering the lawn.

"Are you daft, lass?" he asked, accent thickening with disgust. "It's nearly dusk. Get your arse inside." I hadn't noticed the sky had turned to lavender and pink, the edges burning like tissue paper set on fire. He glowered at Hope. "And you, get inside and close that window. If you run, we have ways of fetching you back. You won't like them."

"I'm not a prisoner," she reminded him gently. "I'm here as a gesture of good faith."

He snorted but didn't answer, preferring instead to nudge me back inside like a great big Scottish bully.

"All right, all right, I'm coming," I muttered. "Someone had to let Mrs. Brown out."

He shut the patio door behind me and locked it. His eyes were smudged with bruises of fatigue. Mrs. Brown chased Byron around the living room until he hid under the library table, whimpering. That, at least, made the night feel more normal. It wasn't long before Liam and Helena came downstairs to join us, followed by Geoffrey, Sebastian, and a rumpled Nicholas. For some reason when he looked at me, I felt myself blushing.

"Still no word from Hyacinth," Helena said grimly and without preamble.

Bruno shook his head, confirming. "We can't track her phone. It's possible she's out of range."

Liam shook his head. "Not likely. I talked to Hart and he claims none of his people came into contact with her."

"And we believe him?" Nicholas asked, leaning back against the mantel and yawning.

Liam's phone rang from the depths of his leather jacket. He answered it, listened, and said only one word. "Good." He looked at his wife. Her shoulders lost some of their tension and then the front door burst open to the rest of the Drake brothers. They rushed in, covered in mud, clothing torn, faces angry.

"Where is she?" Logan asked. "Where's Solange?"

"We don't know," Liam answered him.

Logan closed his eyes briefly, his face pale as lily petals. Quinn swore viciously. Connor punched the wall, denting the plaster.

"Where's your cousin?" Helena frowned, after giving each of her sons the once-over to be sure they were unhurt.

"London took off," Marcus sighed. "She locked one of the grates behind her and just took off."

"What?" Nicholas pushed away from the wall. "You're kidding. She got you into this mess in the first place."

Logan dropped into a chair. "I think she was embarrassed. Or confused. She loves Lady Natasha, you know that."

"And what about Solange?"

"The good news is that Veronique gave her a vial of blood to help her through the change. The bad news is the little idiot gave herself up to the Helios-Ra to save us."

"Not quite," Liam told them starkly. "Your sister gave herself up to a rogue unit currently unrecognized by Helios."

"Well that's just freaking great."

The Drake brothers put a rioting soccer stadium to shame when they got going. And there was nothing like the news that their baby sister had sacrificed herself for them to someone worse than Helios-Ra. The language currently blistering the air would have made the proverbial sailor blush. Helena had to whistle around her thumb and forefinger to make the yelling subside. She was on her feet, her long black braid hanging behind her, her pale eyes like summer lightning.

"Enough. We don't have the time for this." She jabbed a finger at Logan and Nicholas. "You two stay here with Lucy. Sebastian, Geoffrey, your father, and I will find your sister. The rest of you will help Bruno's team find your aunt." She snapped her fingers and it was like a pistol shot. "That's final, not one word out of any of you. Go. *Now*."

The house emptied so fast the silence felt like a slap. I blinked at Nicholas and Logan.

"They don't really think we're going to sit around here and wait, do they?"

"Of course they do," Nicholas replied.

"Look, I'm not sitting around here anymore. Solange needs our help."

"You don't know what you're getting yourself into," Logan said. "You're sixteen and human."

"Shut up."

"I mean it, Lucy. Solange would kill us if we let you put yourself in danger."

"Logan, don't be an ass."

"I have been sleeping in mud. I'm covered in dirt and blood and these were my favorite pants before I landed in raccoon shit."

I bit back a totally inappropriate chuckle. "Raccoon shit?"

"Lucy."

I kissed his cheek, wrinkling my nose. "Why don't you go up and take a shower. If you stop bitching, I'll even wait for you before I figure out what to do next."

He pushed to his feet, groaning like an old man. "I don't think I like you anymore."

I patted his head. "Don't be silly, you love me."

"Try and stay out of trouble in the ten minutes it's going to take me to get clean."

"I can't make any promises," I replied primly.

He shot Nicholas a smirk. "Good luck, little brother."

I scowled at his retreating back.

"What's that supposed to mean?"

CHAPTER 19

♦

Solange

Sunday, sunset

When I opened my eyes, Kieran was crouched next to me, his hand on my shoulder. I jerked back, reflexively. Startled, he did the same.

"Easy," he said. "It's just me."

I blinked, pushing myself up into a sitting position. I felt less like a truck had run over me and then backed up to make sure the job was done properly. Now it felt as if the truck had hit me only once.

"What time is it?" I asked groggily.

"Almost dusk. I tried to wake you earlier but you didn't respond. Scared the crap out of me," he added, muttering as he got to his feet. "I'd rather be well out of here by sundown."

I swung my feet over the edge of the cot.

"Okay, give me a minute." I yawned.

"Whoa." He was staring at me. I resisted the urge to wipe my face to see if there was drool on my cheek or something. "Your eyes."

"What? What?" I scrubbed at them violently, horrified at the thought they might have those gross goopy things at the edges. Or were they even more bloodshot? I'd heard of that happening, where the whites ran with blood.

"I think . . . the color's changing." He paused. "Is that even possible?"

"Is that all? Now you're the one scaring the crap out of me," I muttered back. "Honestly."

"I could have sworn they were darker before you went to sleep."

"They were."

"But they look really blue now."

"They probably are," I replied. "Our eyes get lighter. The really old ones go gray usually."

"Oh."

I shifted uncomfortably. I didn't know how to analyze the way he was looking at me. It made me feel shy and kind of like giggling. And I so was not the giggling type.

"Didn't you want to get out of here?" I asked.

"Yeah." He handed me his jacket, which I slipped on over Lucy's dress. It was torn and stiff with mud up one side. "Are you . . . hungry?"

I froze, looked up at him through my eyelashes. He wasn't offering me blood . . . was he? I tried not to gag.

"I just meant..." His ears went red. "Protein bar?" he explained, pulling one out of his vest pocket.

"Oh." I took it from him, my stomach suddenly rumbling. "Thanks."

We chewed quietly while I tried to figure out what to say to the guy who had tried to kidnap me for money and then within the week saved me from a bunch of his armed brethren. I got that he was doing it for his precious Helios-Ra, to stop the rogue unit before it did serious damage to the league's reputation, but still, I couldn't help but feel as if he might care just a little bit about whether or not I lived through my birthday.

"Can you get us out of here?" he asked once we'd finished our mock chocolate bars. It had settled the hunger pangs but made me thirsty as well. My mouth felt chalky. "Or do we really have to wait until the sun sets?"

"It's easier if we wait, but I think I can turn the alarm off." I raised an eyebrow. "You'll have to turn your back."

He turned slowly. The view from the back was just as good as the view from the front. I could practically hear Lucy snickering in the back of my head. I might be the vampire daughter, but she was the one who was a bad influence. No question. I made sure Kieran wasn't peeking and then cupped my hand over my fingertips as I punched in the code. The light went from flashing red to full red. It was bright enough to have me squinting, my eyes tearing.

"Shit."

"'Shit'? What do you mean, 'shit'?"

"It's okay," I rushed to assure him. "I just used an old code. And, um, set the alarm on freak-out."

He whirled. "Can you shut it off?"

"Of course." I sounded confident for someone who really wasn't. I raced to remember the codes. There was a rotation of a minimum of seven codes, which were changed randomly and continuously. I'd been taught them the way most children were taught their phone number. This should be easy.

The second code didn't work either.

Or the third.

"We're not going to get gassed out of here or something, are we?" Kieran asked nervously.

"Of course not." I paused. "I don't think."

I punched the next code in but my fingers were slippery and slid off the last number. I tried again. The light held red, then went green and blinked off. My shoulders released some of their tension.

"See?" I said nonchalantly. "No problem."

The gate unlocked with a resounding click and I pushed it open. Kieran was close at my back. The smell of damp intensified and then faded, tinged with sunlight and grass. The tunnel led us to a ladder. I paused on the lowest rung.

"Ready?"

"Maybe you should let me go first."

"Forget it." I climbed to the next rung. His hand closed around my ankle. I looked down at him. "Relax, Black. I can climb a ladder."

"What happens when we get up there, Solange?"

"We run like hell until we're home safe and sound? It's a basic plan, but it works for me."

"That rogue unit might still be up there."

"Maybe. But we're coming up pretty far away from where we vanished. And are you telling me they'd hang around for an entire day, just in case?"

"I wish I knew."

"Well, we can't stay here all night."

After a moment, his hold on my ankle released. I could still feel the warm imprint of his palm on my skin as I continued to climb. The trapdoor wouldn't open right away. Kieran had to wedge himself between me and the wall, and we both shoved until the door creaked open. A spear of sunlight landed between us. His eyes were the color of earth—the dark, rich kind you just know will grow the best flowers, the best vegetables. He was very close, close enough that I could see the faint stubble of a beard on his chin and the way his sideburns grew long, shaved to a straight line, the way the men in movies like *Pride and Prejudice* always seem to wear them. It gave him the air of a gentleman pirate. The weapons strapped to his chest didn't hurt. He hauled himself up, never breaking eye contact, even as he snuck past me and managed to be the first one out of the tunnel after all.

"Clear," he called down quietly.

He reached down to grip my upper arms and pulled me up and out, onto the forest floor. The sun filtered softly between the leaves, the shadows long and blue over the ferns and fallen pine needles. Birds sang, oblivious to our presence. There were no footprints in the loam. I stood up, brushing my hands on my dress. Kieran pulled a compass from his pocket, turned it this way and that way.

"There," he said, nodding toward and across a valley of ferns and elder bushes. "Your house is that way. Northwest."

"Thanks." I glanced around awkwardly, glanced back. "I guess this is it, then?"

He frowned. "What are you talking about? I'm not leaving you here alone."

I swallowed, tried to smile. "You have your own stuff to deal with."

"Solange, your eyes are changing color."

"So? What does that have to do with anything?"

"Let me put it this way." He moved so fast, I was impressed despite myself. He shoved my shoulder. I stumbled, hit a nearby oak tree, then tumbled into the mud. My shoulder pulsed painfully.

"Ouch! What the hell was that for?"

"Just proving my point," he told me grimly. "You think I don't see how tired you are? How you're getting weaker?"

I frowned, rubbing my arm. "You pushed me."

"I barely touched you," he pointed out. "And you fell over. I guarantee the rogue Helios-Ra unit will be a lot rougher. Not to mention Lady Natasha's bounty hunters."

I hated that he was right.

"I'm taking you home." He looked stubbornly mutinous. I'd seen that particular expression on every single one of my brothers' faces at one time or another. And there was no gracious way for me to turn him down. No logical, intelligent way, either. He had weapons. I didn't. If someone came at me in the woods, the only thing I could do was yawn them to sleep. And this was the girl Lady Natasha, queen of the vampires, was afraid of.

"Are you coming?" Kieran asked impatiently but with half a smile, as if he knew what I was thinking.

"Okay, but if vamps attack, I want you to run away."

"Sure, right after I pirouette in a pink tutu." He stopped, waited for me to catch up. "Come on, already."

The woods were peaceful and quiet, under the chatter of insects and hidden rabbits and porcupines. Frogs sang from some nearby pond, obscured by the green lace of summer leaves. It might have been romantic if I wasn't convinced someone was waiting around the bend to kill us. He slanted me a glance out of the corner of his eye. And another.

"What?" I asked, without turning my head.

"You're squinting. Do your eyes hurt?"

"A little." I hadn't realized how tightly the muscles around my eyes were scrunched until he mentioned it. My eyes did feel more sensitive, as if the sunlight, even faded the way it was, was hurling needles at my face. I used to love sitting out in the sun with Lucy. It made me a little sad to think we wouldn't be able to do that anymore. Kieran handed me a pair of sunglasses. His fingers brushed mine. He really was kind of sweet for an agent of the cult dedicated to wiping out me and my entire family.

"Are you going to grow fangs too?"

I nearly stopped in my tracks. His hand was still holding mine.

"I guess so." I ran my tongue over my teeth.

"Is your boyfriend worried?"

"I don't have a boyfriend." My smile was ironic. "Kind of hard to bring dates home to meet my parents—and my brothers."

"Good point." His palm pressed against mine. "Watch your step."

We crawled over the exposed roots of a tree that must have fallen in the last storm. It wasn't covered in moss yet or those weird ruffled mushrooms. We climbed down into the valley, as the sun set lower and lower behind the horizon, leaving us in thick, cool shadows. The ground under our feet was soft. There was a wide groove, as if something had slid down to the valley floor.

A scrap of lace trailed from a broken branch in the tangled undergrowth.

My heart stuttered. I felt my hands go clammy before I could even form a coherent sentence. I knew that kind of lace.

"No," I gasped, plucking it like it was a tattered black rose. "No."

I tore down the hillside, slipping in the dirt, skinning my shins and my palms. Pebbles flung up at my passing and pinged me in the legs. Branches scratched my bare arms.

"Solange!" Kieran called, hurrying to catch up. "Wait. Where are you going?"

I slipped and slid the last few feet.

"Be careful!" he hollered behind me.

I barely felt any pain, I was so entirely focused on following the body-wide scrape in the rotted leaves and pine needles.

"Oh my God," I said, spotting a ruffle of lace and ribbon. I'd know those black petticoats anywhere, and the silk corset and jet beads. "Aunt Hyacinth," I called out, crawling closer, tearing ferns out of my way. "Aunt Hyacinth, hold on, hold on."

She was lying on her back, her arm thrown over her face. Her arm from elbow to wrist and the entire left side of her face were blistered and raw. Only her age and the thick shadows of the valley had saved her from the full impact of the sun. Even so, she wasn't moving, wasn't responding at all. I hovered over her, not wanting to touch her in case it caused her more pain.

"Is she . . ." Kieran's question trailed off as he came up behind me, panting for breath.

"I think she's still alive so to speak," I said, swallowing the lump of fear and grief forming in my throat. "She's my aunt." I could practically see bone under the ruin of her cheek. Sunlight alone wouldn't have done that kind of damage. I scowled.

"Holy water," I said through my teeth. "Holy water" was what we called the water Helios-Ra used as a weapon. They charged it with UV rays and vitamin D because we were deathly allergic to it in such concentrated form. "Someone threw holy water on her and then pushed her down the hill. The Helios-Ra use holy water, don't they?" I pressed.

"Solange," he said softly, tightly.

"Don't they?" I yelled.

He nodded once, jerkily. "Sometimes."

"Still so sure your league is totally blameless in everything? Look at her!"

"I'm sorry. I know what it's like to lose family. My father was killed by vampires, remember?"

"I haven't lost her yet," I said grimly, pulling the thick chain out from under my dress. The liquid inside was deep, dark.

"What is that?" Kieran demanded.

"Blood," I said, not looking away from Aunt Hyacinth. I'd never seen her look so frail, so still. It wasn't fair. She'd been hunted because of me, because of the damn bounty on my head. She'd have been safely at home drinking Earl Grey tea or critiquing Lucy's curtsy if it wasn't for me.

"Ancient blood," I explained. "From Veronique Dubois, our matriarch. It has healing properties for anyone of her lineage. I'd give her my blood, but it's tainted right now because of the change."

I didn't mention that my vial held only a single dose, meant to give me an edge even if someone was there to help turn me on my birthday. And no one would be.

I'd see to that.

But first I had to save Aunt Hyacinth. I used my thumbnail to lift the lid, the hinge sticking slightly.

"Hold on, Aunt Hyacinth," I pleaded. "Please hold on. Please, please hold on."

I held the vial to her mouth and tipped it slowly. Blood welled over her lips, filling the crease until it trickled through her teeth and down her chin. She was so pale, nearly blue as her veins struggled to accept the only substance that could save her. Her throat moved slowly, spasmodically.

"She swallowed!" I nearly wept with relief. I held the vial over her mouth until she couldn't swallow anymore. She still didn't open her eyes, didn't talk. But she looked less like she was about to turn to dust. "It's all I can do," I said, letting the chain fall from my fingers. "She needs more, but she's too weak to finish the rest right now. I'll leave the vial with her so that someone can use it to keep her alive if they find her soon enough to revive her."

I rifled through her reticule until I found her cell phone. It had turned itself off when she'd fallen and the plastic was cracked, the screen flickering blue when I finally managed to turn it on. I pressed the code to activate the GPS chip. We weren't that far from the farmhouse. Someone would find her in time.

But I couldn't let them find me.

My brothers had nearly been captured and my aunt was hurt, all because of me. I couldn't bear it if she died or my parents were killed fighting to save me. And Lucy would jump in over her head if she thought it would save me. Even Kieran was putting himself in danger for me and going against his training. I couldn't let any of them sacrifice themselves for me. I just couldn't.

They all wanted to save me, but I just wanted to save them.

And there was only one way to do that. I'd always known it, but I'd hoped I was wrong. Kneeling in the forest with my aunt's burned body convinced me I'd been right all along.

I pulled out my own phone and didn't turn it on, only placed it gently on the ground. And then I smashed it repeatedly with a stone until the case cracked open and the insides were dented beyond repair. I looked up at Kieran, knew my face had gone hard by the way he looked back at me.

"I need your help."

CHAPTER 20

◆

Lucy

Sunday evening

While Logan cleaned up, I took the dogs out again. The gardens were different at night, scraggly and thick. Crickets sang cheerfully from the fields bordering the forest. The moon was yellow and hung in a tatter of clouds like lace. Nicholas was standing guard by the back door and scowling into the darkness. His eyes gleamed.

"Hurry up," he said.

"I can't make the dogs pee any faster." He didn't look at me, turning sharply when something rustled in the bushes. "You look like secret service. All you need is a black suit and shiny shoes."

"I'm just being careful."

"Bruno's out there and we're barely three feet from the door. Besides, no one's after *me*."

"Says the girl with a row of wooden stakes strapped to her chest." He paused. "And are those pink rhinestones?"

"They are," I said proudly. "Who says you can't vanquish in style? And see this one?" I pointed to the stake next to the one I'd decorated with pink rhinestones. It had a skull and crossbones drawn on with black marker. "Pirate theme." He just shook his head at me. I shrugged and tugged on Mrs. Brown's leash when she wriggled her entire front end into a rosebush. Her bottom wagged furiously. "Get out of there," I told her. "Before you get a thorn up your nose."

It took another tug to convince her I was serious. She waddled backward, covered in pink petals. The light from Hope's window above us made a square of yellow on the grass at my feet. It caught on something hanging from the trellis underneath the ledge. I had to stretch up on my tiptoes to reach it. It was a large bronze sun with jagged rays on a leather thong. I plucked it down, wondering if Hope had lost it when she'd hung out the window, trying to convince me to give up the sordid life of a bloodslave.

"Let's go," Nicholas said, opening the door to let the big dogs inside. Mrs. Brown nipped at their heels, grinning her canine grin when they jumped to get away from her. Nicholas ushered me into the safety of the conservatory, his hand on the small of my back. I could feel the coolness of his touch through my shirt. It was dark here as well, full of lilies and orange trees and rare red orchids. A moth fluttered at the glass ceiling, as if the moon were a candle burning over our heads.

Nicholas didn't say anything, and he didn't move away, either. Instead he dipped his head lower, his mouth brushing the skin under my ear and then trailing down to the side of my neck. My head lolled back. Part of me waited for the scrape of teeth, but there was only his lips and his tongue. I was the one who turned slightly and bit gently on his earlobe. His hand pulled me closer against him. It was a struggle to remember why we hadn't gotten along all these years. I couldn't think of a single thing to bicker about.

I couldn't think at all, actually.

I was all warmth and shivers. Night-blooming jasmine sent out sweet tendrils of scent. If I closed my eyes, I could believe we were somewhere exotic, in the jungle or a secret garden in India. I had just slid my arms around Nicholas's neck when the lights flashed on, then off. We froze.

"Alarm," Nicholas whispered. "Someone's opened the tunnel door in the basement."

We hurried down the hall, just as Logan came running down the stairs, his hair still wet, his shirt half-buttoned. There was a shadow in the doorway to the steps leading downstairs. When it stepped forward, it became London, her fangs out as usual. Her hair, usually so strictly slicked down, was a mess of oil-dark spikes.

"You!" I hollered and launched myself at her. My temper burst like a pie left too long in the oven. Nicholas's arm clamped around my stomach, holding me back. I felt like a cartoon character, punching and kicking at air and cursing. London just stood there, pale and quiet. That had me calming down more than Nicholas's struggles to contain me. I'd never seen London when she wasn't sneering at me or shooting her mouth off. She didn't do meekly repentant. It scared me as much as, if not more than, everything that had happened so far.

"I'm fine," I muttered so Nicholas would let go. I pushed my hair out of my eyes.

"Where the hell have you been?" Logan demanded, advancing on London with the kind of fury I'd never thought to see on his pretty face. "We thought you were dead. Or had betrayed us right into that bitch's hands."

"I didn't know," she said softly, wretchedly. "I swear to you, I didn't know." She lifted her chin, expression hardening so that she looked a little more like herself. "Where's everyone?"

"Trying to find Solange," Logan told her. "Who gave herself up to save us all. You included."

"I didn't know Natasha set the bounty. I've served her for years, loved her like a mother. How was I supposed to know? Or do you not remember that she was there for me when the Drakes weren't?" I hadn't heard about this particular blemish on the Drake family tree. I'd just assumed London was crabby all the time because it was in her biological makeup. "She asked me to bring Solange to her, to put an end to any rumors that might start a civil war. And she thinks Montmartre will take her back when there's no threat to her crown."

"Damn it, London," Nicholas muttered.

"I thought I was helping. And I'm oathed to her service, to the royal court." London whirled on him. "What was I supposed to do?"

"Not hand your own cousin over to that bitch, for a start," Nicholas shot back.

London's eyes narrowed. I assumed she was going to launch into a vicious tirade, but instead she took three steps toward me so fast I bumped into the wall behind me trying to get away from her.

Rage poured out of her. If I wasn't immune to her pheromones, I might have passed out at the onslaught. As it was, it made me vaguely light-headed. Nicholas half stepped in front of me.

"Stop it, London."

"Where did you get that?" she demanded. She grabbed the bronze sun hanging from the strap of stakes between my breasts. Her grip was so hard, the bronze dented. I was trapped between her, Nicholas, and the wall.

"I just found it. Get off of me."

"Do you know what this is?"

"No. I found it under Hope's window."

Her pale eyes went pink at the edges. I'd never seen that before. I leaned back to get away from her even though there was nowhere to go.

"Hope? Hope is here?" She whirled, glared at Logan. "Where is she? Where's the Helios bitch?"

"She's an honorable hostage. She doesn't get hurt, Solange doesn't get hurt." Logan blocked the staircase.

"She's a traitor." She said it so quietly I nearly didn't hear her. I did hear her teeth grinding together, however.

"What are you talking about?" Logan demanded.

"I went back to the court after I left you. I still have friends there despite the bounty, friends that will help the Drakes, should it come to that. Hope is double-crossing Helios. She has her own unit, secretly plotting with Lady Natasha. If Hope helps Lady Natasha get rid of Solange and any Drake threat to her throne, Lady Natasha, in return, helps Hope gain control over the Helios-Ra by refusing to treaty with anyone but her."

"Lady Natasha would never treaty with humans," Logan said quietly. "She's always refused."

"Exactly. It would be quite a coup for Helios. And Lady Natasha gets her own human army, ready to wipe out any vampire who doesn't serve her."

"Well, that's just freaking great." Logan jerked his hand through his hair. He blocked London when she tried to dart around him. "You can't kill her," he insisted. "Solange's safety might just depend on it. It was a fair exchange at the time."

"I'm not worried about Solange right now." London snapped the sun disk from the strap, yanking me forward with the sudden momentum.

"Hey!" I stumbled and then straightened, glowering. "Ouch, damn it."

"Do you know what this is?" London yelled at us, holding up the sun. "Do you have any idea?" She tossed it on the floor and spat on it. "This calls Hope's unit to her. They knew she was here—they've known all along."

"She offered herself," I whispered, glancing at Nicholas. "Remember? Hart said he'd stay, but Hope insisted."

"It's a declaration of war," London continued. "It means they're on their way here right now, to set her free and kill anyone in their way. We have to get out of here."

"We can't just hand the farmhouse compound over to them, even saying they can get past Bruno and his crew," Logan said.

"But someone does have to warn the others," Nicholas argued.

"Call them," London said. "But do it fast. We have to get out of here."

"They're in stealth mode. The phones'll be off," Nicholas said. "And I'd bet anything either Mom or Dad or both of them are on their way to the courts right now. You know Dad'll try and talk his way out of the bounty. He'll be walking right into her hands."

Logan pulled his phone out of his pocket.

"Let's at least warn Bruno." He dialed, waited, his mouth tense. His fangs seemed longer, sharper. He hung up after a moment of quiet, clipped conversation. "Good news and bad news." He started up the stairs, taking them two at a time. When the rest followed, I had to grab the back of Nicholas's shirt to keep up. "They found Aunt Hyacinth. Bruno's gone to get her."

"So, we're on our own," London said grimly.

"Aside from the guards. What's that noise?" Nicholas frowned as we rushed down the hall. Boudicca barked loudly, scratching at Hope's door. It took Logan only one kick to break down the door.

The sound was the whirling of helicopter blades.

And Hope was launching herself out of the window, toward the rope. The trees bent, leaves whipping into the room from the force of the wind. The sound of the engine shook the walls. A painting fell off the wall, glass breaking.

Three vampires and a large dog leaped at Hope and not one of them reached her in time.

She swung out of reach, her blond ponytail and strappy sandals incongruous against the helicopter as the armed agents pulled her inside. Arrows rained through the window once she was safely out of the way. An arrow thudded into the bed, three into the floor, another missed Logan's ear only because London shoved him behind the dresser. I leaped toward Boudicca, grabbing for her collar. I tugged her behind the door, Nicholas pushing us both when we weren't moving fast enough for his liking. He cursed the entire time.

"You lunatic, leave the damn dog."

"Shut up, she's a member of this family, too!"

"And she knows how to get out of the way."

"In your family you drink blood. In mine we look after animals."

Boudicca was growling, straining against my grip, trying to get back to the window.

"If you two are done yelling at each other," Logan said drily. "They're gone."

"But the rest are coming," London said. "Ground crew," she added when we just stared at her. "Do you really think they'll let this opportunity pass them by? They know half the family's scattered, looking for Solange or Hyacinth."

"Well, shit."

"Exactly."

"I'll go," Logan declared.

"You can't," I said, chasing him down the stairs.

"I damn well can." He nodded at Nicholas. "Get her in the safe room and lock her in."

"Bite me, Logan," I shot back hotly. "You can't just go barging into the courts, you idiot. You're a Drake, and every bounty hunter in the country is out for your blood."

"So? We can't just let the rest of them go in blind."

"I know that. I'm suggesting you and London stay here and defend the farm."

"And you?" Nicholas asked silkily, suspiciously. "What exactly do you think you'll be doing?"

"Hope was so keen on having me join up with the Helios-Ra," I said, crouching down to pick up Hope's dented sun pendant. "So why don't I?"

CHAPTER 21

♦

Solange

Sunday evening, later

"You look awful," Kieran said.

I would have glared at him but it was taking all of my concentration just to drag one foot in front of the other.

"Stop saying that," I muttered. I hoped I wasn't slurring my words. Even my tongue was tired. Nighttime helped, my metabolism was already stronger when the sun was down. Come morning though, I just knew I'd pass right out. Passing out didn't worry me so much; it was not knowing if I was going to wake up again.

It was nearly my birthday. No party, obviously; no silver-wrapped presents or cake for me—just blood pudding. Gag. I couldn't help but remember my brothers' desperate fights to survive their bloodchanges. They'd weakened so much so fast, it was almost like they were in a coma. It hadn't lasted long, but it hit hard and heavy. Only the elixir of Veronique's blood would give me a fighting edge.

An elixir I no longer had.

I couldn't think about it. It wouldn't do me any good and, anyway, if I had to do it all over again, I would. I stumbled over a tree root, caught myself on an oak branch, and nearly put my own eye out. Kieran caught my elbow. I had to blink rapidly so there was only one of him, not two dancing blurrily with each other.

"You're getting worse."

"If you tell me I look awful again, I am so going to kick you in the shin." I yawned, swayed slightly. "Tomorrow."

"Just try not to fall asleep before you hit the ground. You're harder to catch that way." I knew he was trying to sound confident, but I could smell the worry on him. I could actually smell it, like burned almonds. Weird. I sniffed harder. He raised his eyebrows at me. "Are you smelling me?"

I smiled sheepishly. "Yeah, sorry." I rubbed my nose. "You're worried about me. It smells like almonds."

"Seriously?"

"Yeah. Weird, right?" I sniffed again, frowned. "And I smell stagnant water or mud or something."

"I smell like an old pond?"

I shook my head slowly while my exhausted synapses finally fired straight. My mother's training flooded me, my brothers' stories heard from the privacy of the stairs leading to the attic.

"Not you," I said suddenly. "*Hel-Blar.*"

Kieran froze, but only briefly. "Out here? Now?"

I tried to make my feet move faster. He grabbed my hand and dragged me. *Hel-Blar* weren't to be trifled with. Faintly blue, smelling of rot, with red-tinged eyes and an insatiable appetite for blood. Animal or human, willing or unwilling.

And quiet as bats.

Still, my hearing must be getting sharper even as I grew weaker, because I could hear them skulking between the trees, trailing us, surrounding us like a pack of rabid dogs.

"They're coming," I whispered. "And I can't outrun them like this."

Kieran nodded grimly, swinging an odd-looking gun out of its harness.

"Holy water," he explained. I made sure I was well out of the trajectory of his modified bullets. "Stay behind me," he said needlessly. I was already behind him, using a maple tree to prop myself up, a bouquet of sharpened stakes in my hand. The smell of rotting vegetation and mushrooms was overpowering to my suddenly sensitive nostrils. I gagged.

"They're here."

Their speed alone was terrifying, along with the animal gleam to their eyes. They practically floated, pale as wraiths, slender to the point of being skeletal. Their fangs were sharp and pointed, but so was every other tooth in their head. One of them licked his lips at me.

"Just a taste, princess," he drawled. "You might like it. What do you say?"

I whipped a stake at his chest and he exploded into dust the color of lichen. All vampires crumbled to ash. If I died during the bloodchange, I'd turn to ash too, but it might take a few hours. Uncle Geoffrey claimed it was a Darwinian safety mechanism, to make sure we were never discovered as a species, even after we died.

And this was so the wrong time to be thinking about it.

The others hissed and snarled and all the hairs on my arms stood up. Kieran fired his gun. Light burst like embers whirling through the air, like a carnival trick. Another scent joined the wet rot: singed flesh, burning hair.

"There are too many of them," Kieran grunted. I just grunted back and threw another stake. It missed its mark and was hurled back at us so quickly it pinned the flared hem of my dress to the trunk. Bark flew off in bits, biting into my legs. I swore and yanked myself free.

"Too close," I murmured, nearly tired enough not to care if I fell over and was eaten.

"Stay with me," Kieran snapped, firing again. A *Hel-Blar* flew like a rag doll, crashed into one of his friends. I was already on my knees. That patch of thick ferns looked so inviting. Kieran hauled me up with one arm, still firing with the other.

"You're supposed to run away," I mumbled through a yawn. "You promised."

"The hell I did." He shoved me behind a massive elm tree. "We have to get out of here. Any of your secret gates around here?"

The moonlight was almost as bright as sunlight, searing my pupils. Everything else was blurry. I squinted, tried to make out the shape of the trees around us, the valleys, the location of the river.

"Over there?" I suggested hesitantly. "On the other side of that valley. Maybe."

He kept firing, to give us some cover, and I concentrated on not passing out. Those jagged rocks looked just as comfortable as the ferns. Just a little nap.

"Don't you dare," Kieran said sharply. "You can't sleep yet."

"But I'm so tired."

"Keep moving."

"Wait. The rocks . . ." I rubbed my eyes. "There's a gate behind those rocks."

"Good, get—*ooof*." A dagger bit into his arm, cut through thick leather and skin. Blood welled like plump raspberries. He gritted his teeth. "Just a cut. Keep moving."

I had to crawl through the undergrowth, feeling through the dead leaves for the handle. The iron was cool under my fingers, the rust rough against my palm.

"Got it."

Kieran kicked out at a *Hel-Blar* who was far too close for comfort. He kicked out again, switched his gun for one that shot little vials. The first one hit the ground and broke open, releasing a cross between mist and powder. It was delicate as lace, hovering in the air. I felt funny, entranced by the way it clung to leaves and the *Hel-Blar*.

Hypnos.

"Stop," Kieran commanded grimly. The *Hel-Blar* paused, confused. They hissed frantically but didn't move. I didn't move either. "You," he said to the vampires straining against invisible chains. "You'll get the hell out of here and you won't come back. You'll keep running until you're clear out of the country. And if you try to drink a single drop from any human, you'll walk straight into the next sunrise."

A howl, a grunt.

"Go." They shuffled away. I lay where I was, unable to move. Kieran crouched beside me, his expression regretful but determined,

"I'm sorry," he said.

"Kier—"

"Shhh," he interrupted. "Don't say anything." The Hypnos powder worked through me, making my limbs heavy, my voice falter. "I have to do this, Solange," he murmured. He brushed a kiss over my forehead, gentle as moth wings. Anger and fear burned through me, betrayal was a conflagration that might burn the entire forest to the ground. When I'd suggested he betray me, I hadn't thought he'd take me literally. I'd been a fool to trust him.

And now it was too late.

CHAPTER 22

◆

Lucy

Sunday evening, later still

"I don't know how I let you talk me into this," Nicholas muttered as we ducked into the corridor. "It's a bad idea."

"It's brilliant," I insisted with more certainty than I actually felt. The corridor was damp and cold and confining and hardly gave us an advantage in a fight. But the only alternative was the woods, which were swarming with renegade Helios agents.

Sometimes my life was just weird.

Nicholas stayed close, his arm stretched behind him so that his hand could grip mine. I tugged experimentally. He tugged back.

"I'm losing feeling in my fingers," I complained. He relaxed his hold, infinitesimally. His eyes caught the glow from the torchlight, reflected it like a wolf's eyes might. He wasn't just the Nicholas I'd argued with since I was little, he wasn't even the Nicholas that had kissed me senseless yesterday; he was another Nicholas altogether. The hunter had risen to the surface.

I should probably be worrying about the fact that I was about to walk into the vampire courts instead of staring at his butt. Staring at his butt made me feel less like hyperventilating.

"Breathe," Nicholas murmured, sounding half-strained, half-comforting. "Your heart's not meant to skip beats like that."

I wiped my free hand on my pants, hoping the palm he was holding wasn't as sweaty. I'd changed into a pair of Solange's cargos, assuming they looked more like something a secret agent would wear than my velvet skirts and beaded scarves. There was clay all over the left leg. It made me feel like crying for some reason. I was trying so hard not to imagine the hundreds of horrible things that might have happened to my best friend. She had to be safe. Absolutely nothing else was acceptable. Nicholas's thumb made small soft circles over my knuckles. I released my pent-up breath. My eyes stopped burning. We could do this. We *had* to, it was that simple.

"I'm okay," I whispered.

"I—" He cut himself off, squeezed my hand once, hard. My heart stopped, then leaped into overdrive. I couldn't hear anything except the blood rushing in my ears and the drip of water, even though I was listening as hard as I possibly could. He sniffed once. I tensed all over; even my eyelids felt tight. He held up three fingers. Since he wasn't speaking, not even a whisper, I assumed it was vampires.

Footsteps were suddenly audible and they were incredibly close. I reached for one of my stakes, wondering suddenly if I was really going to be able to stick it into someone's chest. As a theory it worked fine; as an actual attempt to shove a hunk of whitethorn wood through bone and flesh and heart, I wasn't so sure. In any case, I didn't have the time to consider my options. Nicholas pushed me against the damp wall. His hand fisted in my hair and tugged my head until my neck was exposed. He ripped off the Drake cameo I'd forgotten to take off. His eyes met mine, his lips lifting slowly off his teeth. His canines were sharp, long, and gleaming like pearls. I wasn't quite as immune to his pheromones as I'd assumed. I was mesmerized, and he pressed even closer to me.

And then we weren't alone anymore.

I could tell he knew the moment the hall disgorged the three vampires, but he didn't turn or freeze or give himself away. He only dragged his mouth over the arch of my bare neck until I shivered. My crossbow was slung back, hanging behind me.

"Hey." One of them snickered.

Nicholas kept his back to them—risky, but not as risky as giving himself away as one of the Drake brothers. His teeth scraped my throat. I shivered again.

"Busy," he drawled at them. "Get your own."

"No time to have a drink," they replied. "Hunting the Drakes. Seen any?"

Nicholas shrugged one shoulder.

"At the farmhouse, usually. Second door around the corner will get you out into the woods." And straight into the eager, waiting arms of Hope's agents.

"Thanks."

He only grunted, nibbling my ear. My hair fell over his face, veiling his features. We stayed as we were until even he couldn't hear the receding footsteps anymore. He pushed away from me as if it was the hardest thing he'd ever done. His jaw was clenched so tightly, the muscles in his cheek jumped.

"That was close," he ground out.

I nodded, trying to catch my breath. "Thank God they were in such a hurry."

"That's not what I meant," he whispered.

"Oh." I stayed where I was, even as he leaned against the opposite wall, jerking his hand viciously through his hair. "Are you okay?"

"Let's just get this over with," he growled.

"How are we going to find your parents?" I asked as we started jogging down the corridor.

"If they're not already at the courts, they should be in the woods just outside. This way." He pushed open a grate in the ceiling and made a stirrup out of his linked hands for me to step up into. I leaped, he threw, and I landed half in the dirt with my legs dangling. I scrambled out of the way. He shot up out of the earth, landing in a graceful crouch. He tossed his hair off his face.

"Let's go."

The wind was warm, pushing its way between the leaves, but there were no other sounds—not a single cricket chirping or a rabbit dashing for safety. I walked as carefully as I could, trying not to break any twigs to give away our location. The mountain crouched over us, solid and filled with secrets. I used to worry about bears this far into the wild, not vampire queens.

We ran for a while, until I had to stop, panting, and rest against an elm tree. My lungs burned and sweat soaked my hair. I pressed a hand to my chest.

"Just a minute," I gasped. "Just a minute."

Nicholas looked around, nostrils flaring.

"Nothing," he said, his fists clenching. "I can't smell them anywhere—it's all Lady Natasha and her damned Araksaka." He slapped at a low-hanging branch. "Solange doesn't have any time left."

"I know," I said quietly. "But she's stronger than you think."

"Not during the bloodchange. She'll be out cold."

"Even then," I insisted stubbornly. "You don't know her like I do."

"Lucy." He looked beaten. "Listen, you have to face—"

"No," I interrupted fiercely. "*You* listen. We will find her. We will save her. Period. Okay?" I blinked back tears, fighting a bubble of hysteria in my throat. "Okay?"

He stepped closer, and I had to wipe my eyes so he wasn't blurry.

"Shh." He touched my cheek very gently. "Okay, Lucy. Okay."

I pushed away from the tree even though my legs still felt like jelly. "So we keep looking."

He looked at me for a long moment and then nodded. "If Mom's planning to attack the courts, she'll do it through the side entrance there. No one ever uses it anymore. If they're not there, we'll leave a message for them."

I armed my crossbow. He winced.

"Careful with that thing."

"Yeah, yeah."

We climbed through the brush, using tree roots as handholds, scattering pebbles underfoot no matter how carefully I stepped. The entrance was blocked with rocks.

They weren't there.

Nicholas didn't lose his temper again, only crouched and made marks on the rock with the edge of a broken stone. There were no marks already there, waiting for him to decipher. His parents hadn't been this way after all.

"And if your dad was the one with the plan?"

"Then he'll already be in there, talking treaties."

"They might still be looking for Solange, might have found her and brought her home."

"Maybe."

"So what do we do now?"

"Plan B."

I stared at him, the back of my neck prickling. "Plan B?"

He nodded grimly. "Royal guard, coming from the west."

"Shit." I fumbled for the set of handcuffs we'd found in the weapons room. We'd made sure to open the links in the chain that secured them together so he could break free if our plans went awry, which they already had. He held out his wrists and I snapped them shut. I, at least, got to keep all of my weapons, though he had made me hide my pink rhinestone stake. I added a swagger to my walk. I was pretty sure all Helios-Ra agents learned the swagger along with how to sharpen their weapons and the proper way to apply holy water.

"Why are you limping like that?" Nicholas demanded.

"I'm swaggering," I informed him.

"You look like you're wearing a diaper."

Charming. And I had a crush on this guy.

Wait.

I had a crush on this guy?

"Now what?" he asked. "You're making weird faces."

"Nothing," I said quickly. "Never mind." One crisis at a time.

Speaking of a crisis.

Two of Natasha's Araksaka came at us, quick as wasps. The insignia of Natasha's house was tattooed over the left side of their faces: three detailed raven feathers. One was a huge oiled man who belonged on the set of *Conan the Barbarian*. The other was a petite black-haired woman whose smile was feral enough to make my palms sweat again.

"Who are you?" she demanded.

"I'm here to collect the bounty," I announced, my voice cracking only slightly. I tossed my hair off my face in a way I hoped looked cool and nonchalant and not like a nervous tic, which it most definitely was. The woman sniffed, narrowed her eyes.

"Human."

"Go away, little girl," the man said brusquely. "You don't want to come in here."

The woman took a step closer. "Humans don't collect bounties," she snarled. "Helios."

I moved the crossbow slightly, still keeping it at the level of her chest. Moonlight glinted off the dented sun pendant around my neck. "I'm with Hope, actually."

Something flickered in their faces but I couldn't read it. She jerked her head in a nod for us to follow. I poked Nicholas in the shoulder with the crossbow.

"Move it," I ordered. He walked slowly in front of me and I tried not to look as if I was nervous enough to drop my crossbow and shoot myself in the foot. Which was a distinct possibility.

It took forever to climb down and around to the cave entrance. Two more guards waited at the door. They didn't say a word, barely glanced at us. Halfway down a damp tunnel, a woman with long curly hair stepped into view, and several more guards came up behind us. They bowed, but only quickly, so I guessed she wasn't Lady Natasha. I expected the queen of the vampire tribes might not pout so peevishly. But then I'd never met royalty, vampire or otherwise.

"Is this a Drake boy?" She sniffed once, disdainfully. "Pretty enough, I grant you, but hardly seems worth all the fuss."

"Juliana, go away," the female guard snapped impatiently.

Juliana frowned. "You should be more polite. I am the queen's sister, after all."

"Go away, *my lady*," the guard amended. "Lady Natasha's orders are to keep you safe."

"I hardly think these children are a danger to me," she said scornfully, but she eventually drifted away. The rest of the guards pressed behind me. The silence stretched, like a bowstring about to snap. I knew the rules: show no fear. And I couldn't just wait around until they decided to rip out my throat.

"Look, are we going to stand around here all night staring at each other? I want my reward."

"This way."

Actually, standing around was starting to have some appeal.

The damp cavern gave way to an arched stone hallway lit with oil lamps set into deep crevices. The dirt floor became flagstone layered with Persian rugs as we went deeper into the labyrinthine caves. The Araksaka fanned out, three in front, three in back. I felt like I was in the middle of a particularly tense vampire sandwich.

Shadowed figures coalesced in the dark openings to watch us pass. Eyes and teeth gleamed menacingly. By the time we reached the central cave, which was surprisingly tall, with jeweled stalactites, a crowd of pale-eyed vampires waited for us. Quartz glittered in the walls between hand-embroidered tapestries showing various events in vampire history and lore. There was a lot of red thread. The furniture was an eclectic mixture of antiques passed down through the centuries. It was mostly old wood, with a smooth patina of age, accented with a few modern pieces here and there.

I was trying really hard not to focus on the hissing. Even growing up around the Drakes wasn't quite enough to immunize me to that many vampires. The air was so thick with pheromones that adrenaline poured through my bloodstream. I felt a little drunk and edgy with it. More than one vampire licked his lips, staring at me like I was chocolate mousse cake. I lifted my crossbow threateningly. The vampires eased back, but only barely.

There were mirrors everywhere. There were massive ones in gilded frames, tall cheval glasses, small broken shards glued to the wall. And in the center of the cavern, there was a single throne made of whitethorn wood, the kind that makes the best stakes, carved into dozens of pale crows. Every feather was painstakingly detailed, and their obsidian eyes glittered in the torchlight. Sitting on the throne, smiling faintly, was Lady Natasha. She was beautiful, of course, and dramatic, with long, straight blond hair. Her bangs were cut straight over arched brows and pale blue eyes so light they appeared nearly translucent. She was slender and as white as a birch sapling.

"And what have we here?" she murmured, sultry as a long summer night. Her voice held back the ocean of tension as if it were a cup of water. "Hansel and Gretel, lost in the woods?"

Soft laughter draped over us like fur blankets. I locked my knees together so they wouldn't shake.

"I've come for the bounty," I announced. "I've captured a Drake."

"Have you now?" One of her guards handed her a glass goblet filled with blood. She took a dainty sip, dabbed at her lips with a square of lace. "And you are?"

"I'm with Hope."

"I see." She tilted her head. "Arrogant smirk, lovely cheekbones. Yes, this is definitely one of Liam's spawn."

"Go to hell," Nicholas spat.

"And Helena's spawn as well, clearly. Abominable manners."

"The bounty?" I asked, my brain racing frantically. We needed to leave this main hall with its crowds of vampires, but I didn't know how to get us out of there.

Lucy

And then it went from bad to worse.

Much, much worse.

Kieran Black stalked toward us, trailing guards. His face was all angles, his smile sharp and insolent. In his hands he held a wooden box inlaid with pearls. Before any of us could move or even speak, he flipped open the lid.

Inside, a heart dripped blood through the iron hinges.

"The heart of Solange Drake," he announced. "Your Majesty."

CHAPTER 23

◆

Lucy

Everything stopped.

I couldn't bring myself to look away from the red lump bleeding in the delicate box. The pearls went pink under the oozing blood. Nausea rolled in my stomach. I couldn't form a coherent thought, couldn't move, could barely breathe.

Not Solange. Not Solange.

Kieran stood like any good soldier, looking straight ahead, blood dripping at his feet. He was muddy and tired, his sleeves pushed up to display his Helios-Ra tattoo. I had never physically hated anyone in my entire life the way I hated him now.

"No," I finally choked out. "It's not possible."

"So many gifts," Lady Natasha murmured, rising gracefully to her feet.

And then, chaos.

"My baby sister," Nicholas yelled, leaping into the air, fangs extended, snapping his handcuffs apart. He aimed at Kieran's throat, his eyes like silver coins. Lady Natasha raised an eyebrow, and it was as if she'd let out a battle yell. Araksaka closed in from all directions so quickly their feather tattoos seemed to flutter.

"Nicholas, behind you!" It wasn't enough to help him in any way, but it was just enough to give ourselves away entirely. I was hardly part of Hope's unit if I was trying to save my Drake captive. And I did try. I went to pull one of my stakes from its sheath, but it was as if I were moving in slow motion and everyone else was in fast-forward, like those nature documentaries where an orchid blooms and wilts in three seconds. Only we were trapped in a garden of vampires, blooming like deadly nightshade and belladonna and thirsty for our blood.

Nicholas didn't land as he'd planned, thrown off course by the flying granny boot of an Araksaka, which caught him full in the chest. Kieran went into a roll and came up several feet away, bloody heart rolling across the floor. I gagged as it came to a soggy halt near my left foot. I was shaking and choking on the bile in my throat and absolutely no match for the guards who grabbed me.

"Get off her." Nicholas struggled as he was hauled to his feet, nose bleeding sluggishly. Kieran wouldn't look at me. Lady Natasha flicked her hand.

"Such drama," she said, as if we were a dinner show that bored her.

For all I knew, we *were* the dinner show.

And dinner, for that matter.

"I haven't time for children," she said. "There are still preparations to be made for the ball tomorrow night." She patted a stool next to her throne. "Have a seat near me, dear boy." She smiled at Kieran, showing teeth like polished shells. "We have much to celebrate. Civil war has been averted, thanks in part to you."

"I only want the money."

I spat at him. I couldn't help it. I was immobilized between two Araksaka and there was nothing else I could do.

At the moment.

Because, karmic baggage or not, if I got through this alive, I was going to break more than his nose.

Lady Natasha sniffed with distaste. "Barbaric." She waved a hand. "Take them away, won't you? They're becoming tiresome."

Nicholas and I were dragged out of the plush hall. I was shorter than my captors and my feet dangled slightly off the ground. The stairs were narrow and damp, cut roughly out of the stone and leading into more damp and more darkness. One of them shoved me, and I stumbled down the last few steps, landing hard on my hip. I could hear Nicholas struggling, cursing.

"Lucy! Lucy, are you okay?"

"I'm fine," I forced out, once my breath returned. "Ouch!" I was hauled back up to my feet and none too gently. The stairs had led us down to dungeons. Actual dungeons, carved out of rock, with slick iron gates and the chitter of rats. "This is so not good," I muttered, fear making me mouthy as usual. "You can't seriously think you can keep us here. We have friends, you know, angry friends. And you're serving a paranoid selfish—urk." My tirade was cut abruptly short by a hand to my throat. I couldn't even swallow, couldn't breathe, could only feel my face turning purple. I tried to make a sound, scratched at the unbending fingers. The eyes that met mine were cold, flat. And then I was sailing backward into a cell, hitting the wall with enough force to make me see stars. I slumped, gasping. Nicholas was shoved into the only other cell, across from me.

"My family will come," he promised darkly.

"As it should be," the guard said. "The Drake clan will witness the final crowning of Lady Natasha, with none to usurp her throne."

"Solange didn't even want your stupid crown," I croaked through my bruised throat. "Or your throne."

"She was a threat, now she's not."

I opened my mouth to yell. I was angry and bereft and afraid and all of those things made my temper harder to control than usual. Nicholas's eyes flared at me warningly. He was right. I could swear and fume all I wanted, it wouldn't change anything. And I was already bruised all over, and we'd been here less than a half hour. I wasn't exactly a force to be reckoned with. I slumped against the wall and held my tears until the royal guard had filed out and we were alone with the cold drafts and the mildew. Sobs finally racked through me and I couldn't stop them. They were loud and ugly, not like movie tears, which always seem so delicate and fragile. My tears burned and stung and didn't make me feel the slightest bit better.

I'd known Solange all of my life. Sometimes I knew her better than I knew myself. She was solitary and clever and elegant even when she was adamant that was she was no such thing. She was special, and not just because she was the only vampire daughter.

She was loyal and had always been there for me, no matter what. She was the one who nursed me through countless ill-advised crushes; she was the one who snuck me ice cream when my parents discovered tofu desserts and wouldn't buy anything else. She was quiet and strong and artistic.

It was unthinkable that she was dead.

I gagged on more tears. It wasn't right. This wasn't how it was supposed to happen. We were supposed to be at her house, where she'd drink her first taste of blood at midnight tonight and wake up sixteen years old and dead—or reborn, technically, whatever. Not this. Never this.

"Lucy." Nicholas pressed against the iron bars. I had no idea how long he'd been saying my name. I was curled into a ball, my eyes swollen. I wiped my nose on my sleeve.

"Sorry," I said, blinking away the last of the tears. More hovered behind my lids, clutching at my throat, but I had to fight them back. It wasn't in me to just give up, even when I desperately wanted to. I couldn't force a smile, but at least I could sit up. Nicholas looked worried and wretched. "What are we going to do?" I asked.

His fists clenched around the bars.

"We're going to get out of here somehow. They're going to take us up to the hall for the ball. Lady Natasha wants to gloat and show the vampire clans that she's defeated the Drakes. It's posturing."

"I really hate her."

"I know."

"No, I mean, like, a lot."

"Me too."

"And Kieran, that rat." My voice caught. "I'm going to break his nose again. And the rest of him."

"I'll help."

"My mom's going to make me spend weekends at the ashram for the next ten years to cleanse me of all this violence if we survive."

"*When* we survive," he corrected. He was pale, almost misty in the flickering light of the single torch on the wall between us. Smoke hung near the low ceiling, darkening the stones. "Dawn's not far off," he said, frustrated. His eyes looked bruised, even from a distance. "I won't be able to stay awake much longer." He sat on the ground, leaned his head back on the wall. "I'm sorry I wasn't able to protect you."

"Right back at you."

He half smiled. "Don't shoot your mouth off while I'm asleep."

"I can't make any promises."

"My family *will* come," he said again.

I thought of Liam's grim face, of Helena's sword flashing.

"I can't wait."

CHAPTER 24

◆

Solange

I lay there for a long time. I could have been there hours, days, months; I'd lost track. There was only my breath becoming longer and deeper and slower. I felt like a dandelion gone to fluffy white seed, drifting on the wish of some petulant child. I hoped my family was safe, tucked into the old farmhouse. I'd miss its crooked halls and creaky floors and my little pottery shed with its views of the fields and the woods and the mountains beyond. I'd miss Nicholas nagging at me to be careful, Lucy arguing with everyone about everything, Kieran's quiet confidence.

At first I thought I'd imagined the faint clang.

But the voices were real, echoing down to my bed. I tried to move, to open my eyes, but nothing happened.

"This is the one," someone said. The voice was rough. "I can smell her."

"Aye, like bloodwine just waiting to be sipped."

The footsteps approached. I managed to pry one eye open, not enough that anyone would notice, just enough that the faint light showed me two men and a woman through the fringe of my lashes. Each of their faces was tattooed with the three raven feathers of the royal house.

Araksaka.

I tried harder to move, to scream, to kick out. It was as if I was barely in my body—it paid virtually no attention to my frantic commands.

"Not quite out yet, are you sweetheart?" I tried to fight but only dangled limply over his arms when he picked me up. His mouth was very near my neck. I shuddered violently. "Just a little taste."

"Michel, no." Someone plucked me away like an apple off a tree. "Lady Natasha would have your head," he said. "And more importantly, mine as well."

"But she smells so delicious."

"Put in your damn nose plugs—you know it's the bloodchange pheromones."

"Spoilsport."

"If you two are quite finished courting," the woman snapped, looking down as she climbed the rope back up to the forest floor. "We don't have much time."

My captor slung me over his shoulder and went up the rope, quick as a hummingbird. The light in the woods was faintly gray, the sky like a black pearl. I could feel the approach of dawn, the way I'd never actually felt it before. It was like a weight on my chest, like being wrapped in chains and dropped into the ocean.

The guards felt it just as keenly as I did, I could tell by the way they lowered their heads and ran faster than I'd ever seen a vampire run. The trees blurred into shadows, the leaves slapping at us faintly as we passed. Coyotes yipped hysterically from the valley behind us. The mountain loomed closer and closer, blocking out the shimmer of light on the horizon. The woman cursed. They ran faster. I hoped they crumbled into ashes, even if it meant I would too.

And then we were at the caves and they leaped inside as if their feet were on fire. The first spear of sunlight hurled from the sky, fell between the branches and struck the ground. It gilded the humus underfoot, the curling ferns, the white birch bark peeling into strips. The woman cursed again.

"Too damn close."

That would be my very last moment of sunlight. Ever. My skin itched all over. I was certain that if I'd been caught out there, I would have blistered as badly as the other vampires would have.

I was taken down a narrow tunnel and into a circular hall with rugs on the floor and tapestries on the walls. Torches burned and candles were scattered everywhere, like stars on a clear winter night. Ravens cawed from floor to ceiling in wrought-iron cages, eyes gleaming like jet beads. The few vampires there stopped what they were doing and followed us to a white throne, trailing behind us like the train of a wedding dress. Lady Natasha was on her feet, her face so pale it could have been carved out of moonstone. Even her hair seemed stunned, white as orchids. I might have enjoyed that brief moment of victory, if I hadn't seen Kieran beside her, equally pale. What was he still doing here? Our plan was falling apart around us and there wasn't a single thing I could do about it.

"Is that Solange Drake?" Lady Natasha's voice was cold enough to crack steel. I couldn't quite place her accent. It seemed vaguely French, vaguely Russian.

The guard still carrying me lowered himself to one knee.

"Yes, my lady. We found her in the woods."

"Did you now?" She turned her head a fraction of an inch toward Kieran. He was staring at me, so many emotions chasing across his face that I didn't have time to decipher them all.

Our plan hadn't worked after all.

Natasha gestured to a silver plate on which lay a roasted heart, swimming in a pond of blood. The pearl-studded iron box Kieran had taken from the chest before leaving me to go hunting sat nearby. "And what, pray tell, is this delicacy I was about to consume?"

Kieran didn't answer, didn't look away from me as I was released to tumble to the carpet.

"I asked you a question, boy." One backhand and Kieran was crashing into the table, scattering a vase of roses, a crystal bowl, and the silver plate. The heart hit the side of the throne and slid slowly down in a syrupy trail of blood. I would have gagged, but even my throat was too tired from the bloodchange to react. Kieran coughed, rubbing his chest as he pushed himself up into a sitting position.

"It's a deer heart," he replied without inflection.

"How very clever," she purred. One of the royal guards winced at the sound. She raised an eyebrow at the guard still on one knee.

"We've much to do apparently. The ball will go on as planned, and we'll set the Drake girl up on the dais so that everyone can watch her die, along with any threat to our unity."

"No." Kieran leaped to his feet.

She smiled at him.

"And you'll watch every moment of it, after which, I will pull your heart out of your puny rib cage and eat it. Seeing as I was denied my treat."

"Solange doesn't want your throne or Montmartre," Kieran insisted, crouching to put his back to a tapestry of a maiden drinking from a white unicorn, when two guards began closing in on him. "She doesn't want to be queen of the damn vampires."

"Don't be stupid." Lady Natasha paused, turned to the doorway. She sighed. "Now what? I don't recall inviting you."

"There's been a change of plans." Hope marched into the room, two agents behind her. Her eyes narrowed. "Kieran. What the hell are you doing here?"

Natasha lifted her chin.

"Kieran?" she repeated icily. "As in the son of Hart's brother? When you killed him you said you had everything under control."

Kieran froze. He looked as if he was going to choke on his fury.

"What?" He turned slowly toward Hope. "What did she just say?"

"Everything is under control, but I hardly expected you to invite a Helios agent into your court."

"He brought me a heart." Lady Natasha nodded toward me. I was still sprawled on the carpet. "Clearly not hers."

"Well, the Drakes are on to me now," Hope snapped.

CHAPTER 25

•

Lucy

Monday morning

I must have dozed off, even though the thought of it seemed impossible. The sound of the iron lock opening woke me up. I was on my feet before my eyes were even fully open. It was the *Conan* extra who had led us into the hall yesterday. His muscles were even bigger close up, but he looked a little haggard. I had no idea how long I'd slept, but Nicholas was out cold in his cell, didn't even stir at the sound of the iron gate swinging open on rusty hinges. I might have tried to dart around the guard but he was big enough to block the entire space and, anyway, where would I go? Up the stairs into the main hall?

He placed a jug of water on the floor. "You should clean up."

I frowned. "What? Why?" For some reason I thought his voice

"You," Kieran bit out, fists clenching.

Hope didn't look particularly concerned with the hatred pouring out of him.

"I'm doing what I have to for the Helios-Ra, and I guarantee it's more than your father or uncle could ever have accomplished. Lady Natasha understands that. We look after our own."

Kieran didn't bother with more debate; he launched himself at her. He didn't make it within two feet of her, of course, not with her men there and the Araksaka as well. He didn't have a chance. I doubt that mattered to him.

"Honestly, children these days." Natasha waved her hand, looking bored. "Take them away."

sounded familiar, but I was pretty sure I would have remembered him if I'd seen him before.

"It's expected."

"Well, you can take your—"

"Stay down," he advised quietly. "And keep your mouth shut."

Was he actually trying to help me? The apple he tossed me nearly hit me in the face. I caught it mostly by reflex. Then I realized why I recognized his voice. He was the vampire who'd come to the window of the farmhouse and offered his allegiance.

He straightened at the sound of footsteps on the stairs. His expression went hard, blank. Two women came up behind him, not tattooed with the mark of Araksaka but not exactly friendly, either. They brought in a basket and a beautiful gown, all brocade and embroidered velvet with a square neckline and panniers and lace petticoats. It was burgundy with pale blue crystal beads and accents on the bodice and around the hem. The dress's hanger was placed on a hook intended for iron chains and other methods of torture.

Now I was really confused.

That the basket was filled with a silver-backed hairbrush, a hand mirror, a square of lavender soap, and vials of perfume didn't clear things up even a little.

"Um . . . what is all this stuff?"

The women eyed me critically.

"It should fit. The shoes look too small, you'll have to go barefoot."

"I'm supposed to wear that costume?" At any other time, I would have been thrilled to prance around in some old-fashioned gown dripping with ornamentation.

"You can't very well attend a ball in those dirty things, can you?" She sneered at my pants. "It would be an insult to our queen."

I felt staggered. I actually pressed a hand to my temple.

"Wait, it's an actual ball? Waltzing and canapés and glass slippers?" My very first ball and it was in honor of a lunatic murderer and would likely end with a vampire killing me. And I had to dress up for the pleasure?

"Don't get the dress dirty," one of them said.

"Why not?"

"Lady Natasha would be . . . displeased."

"This is totally surreal," I muttered after they'd left me alone with my very own ball gown. There was a zipper up the side, so at least I wasn't expected to contort myself around to do up my own laces. Hyacinth had always said the reason well-to-do ladies had maidservants was because none of the clothes were user-friendly. The gown was beautiful, embellished by hand, every minute detail perfectly done. And I didn't want to wear it, not one bit. I edged back as if were dipped in poison.

Instead of using the water in the jug to wash with, I drank every drop. I was thirsty and hungry enough that my stomach cramped around the apple I ate. I paced a while because I literally had no idea what else to do with myself. This was the last situation I'd ever expected to be in. I was at a complete loss.

"Nicholas," I called out. He was on his back, still as stone. "Nicholas," I tried again. Nothing. Not a flicker of an eyelash. I gave up and went back to pacing. After an hour of pacing, my calves were sore and I was feeling dizzy. I used the chamber pot, while I knew Nicholas was still asleep, and then decided to put the dress on when I realized that if the guards came down and I was still in Solange's cargos, they'd likely strip me down themselves. A white cotton slip dress went on first, followed by the panniers, which were basically two baskets hanging on a wide leather belt that went around my waist. It felt weird and bulky. The dress went on top and was heavier than it looked. The fabric was stiff and tight enough that I had no choice but to stand up straight. There was a blue velvet choker. I wished I still had the Drake family cameo; I'd attach it out of spite.

And it might give me courage.

Because I talked a good game, but the truth was, my knees were weak as water and I felt sick to my stomach. Panic was stealthy and it hunted me on soft, silent feet, not quite closing in but never going away, either.

So when Conan returned, I really thought that I was hallucinating.

Kieran was thrown into Nicholas's cell, his face bloody and bruised, his left arm hugged to his chest as if it was broken. But what really caught my attention was the body draped over Conan's huge arms, gently placed on the pallet beside me.

Solange.

CHAPTER 26

♦

Lucy

It was surprisingly difficult to crouch down by Solange's side, and not just because of the ridiculous dress. Her head lolled to one side as if even her neck was too tired to hold it up. I couldn't tell if she was breathing, and my hands shook as I leaned closer. I really didn't want to see a gaping hole in my best friend's chest. I wouldn't just dirty Lady Natasha's dress, I'd throw up all over it.

"It wasn't *her* heart," Kieran groaned from his cell. "It was a *deer* heart."

"Shut up," I shot back. "I don't know if I'm talking to you yet." I touched Solange's shoulder. She was cool and covered in mud. "Solange?"

"It's the bloodchange."

"I said shut up," I tossed over my shoulder. "I know what it is, she's my best friend, isn't she?" I narrowed my eyes. "And you look like shit."

"Arm's broken," he agreed. He looked gray, hollowed. "Hope killed my dad."

"I told you it wasn't the Drakes." I wrinkled my nose. I could hear my dad in my head, going on about compassion. "And I'm sorry. Not that I don't still want to wring your neck."

"I had to be believable, for all the good it did. Hope's up there. She gave me away."

"Want me to break her nose?"

"Hell, yes."

"I'll add it to my list."

"What are you and Nicholas doing here anyway?"

"Hope," I told him. "She escaped and sent her unit in to take over the farmhouse. Nicholas and I made it out. We were hoping to warn his parents off but we couldn't find them. And they're still out there looking for Solange."

"I'm sure they're here or near enough anyway. They don't strike me as the type to stay out of the action for long."

"That's true," I said, buoyed. I turned back to Solange. "Thank God, she's alive. When she wakes up I'm going to kill her." I brushed her hair back. "If you can hear me, Sol, you better come through this. I know you can do it. Your namby brothers did it, so you can, too." I draped my discarded sweater over her. "What the hell was she doing, anyway?" I asked Kieran.

"She was running away."

"No way."

"We found Hyacinth."

My heart dropped. "Is she . . . ?"

"She should survive, if they got her home quickly enough."

"Assuming there's still a home, of course. Hope's got it in her crosshairs."

He shifted, swore when he bumped his arm. I tossed him my belt since I wasn't sure he'd be able to get his own off. Nicholas was still lying in a heap in the corner.

"Here, set your arm."

"Thanks." Sweat beaded his forehead as he worked to wrap the belt around his shoulder. He looked like he knew what he was doing. "Do a lot of battlefield medicine, do you?"

"You've met the Drakes."

"Good point."

I watched him struggle and sighed irritably. "I guess I don't hate you after all."

"I tried to save her." He pulled the belt tight with his teeth. Lines of pain etched around his mouth. "She was supposed to be safe underground."

"Everything's such a mess," I mumbled.

"It's worse than you think."

"Of course it is." I rubbed my face. "I'm afraid to ask, I really am." At least my panic seemed to have desensitized itself.

"Lady Natasha wants to watch Solange die as the entertainment for her freakin' ball."

I ground my teeth. "Oh, I *don't* think so." I reached for the vial of Veronique's blood Logan had said she was wearing around her neck. I frowned, lifted her head to see if it had fallen behind her. "Where's the vial? Kieran, where is it?"

"She used it to save Hyacinth."

"What?" I let her head drop, none too gently. "It's the only thing that could have saved her." I slapped the ground. "You know what this means?" I asked grimly.

"What?"

"Lady Natasha might just get her wish."

◆

Monday evening

When Nicholas finally woke up, it wasn't pretty. He went from unconscious to hyperalert so fast I missed the transition.

"You bloody bastard." His eyes flashed as he stalked him. "You killed my sister!"

"Wait—," Kieran screamed when Nicholas grabbed his broken arm. He kicked out, aiming for Nicholas's knees. There was a grunt, more sounds of fists and feet hitting flesh.

"Nicholas!" I shouted through the bars. "Nicholas, stop it."

"He killed Solange."

"No, he didn't." Kieran was dangling off the ground, his face going purple. "Put him down."

"He has to pay."

"Nicholas Drake."

He didn't let go, but he did finally turn to look at me. I pointed to Solange, on her back on the pallet. He dropped Kieran so fast, Kieran stumbled.

"Solange? Solange!"

"She hasn't moved since they brought her here."

He finally grinned, looking like the Nicholas I remembered from the Christmas Eve he got his first bike. "She's not dead!" He frowned. "Why don't you look happier?"

"She gave her vial away."

"She gave her . . . son of a bitch."

I leaned my forehead on the cold bars.

"Today just sucks." I tried for a smile. "On the plus side, I get to see you prance around in tights."

Only his eyebrow moved, but it was enough. "I beg your pardon?"

I pointed to the pile of clothes on the ground by his foot. "Your formal wear."

He glanced at it, then back at me. "Nice dress. Can you breathe in that thing?"

I smoothed the front of my dress. "It would be much more fun to wear if it wasn't what I was going to be buried in."

"You are not going to be buried." He paused, lifted the clothes up suspiciously. "Vampires don't bury their victims," he added distractedly.

"Hey, looking for comfort here."

"Sorry." He shook out the doublet, complete with lace froth at the cuffs. "Logan would love this." He smirked at me. "No tights." He dropped everything. "I'm still not wearing this crap."

"They seemed rather adamant."

"She can kiss my—hey." He scowled at Kieran. "There's only one costume. How come you don't have dress up like some eighteenth-century jackass?"

Kieran was still cradling his arm, his hair damp with sweat.

He looked wan but still managed to smirk back. "I'm not a prince from the illustrious Drake family."

"Cut it out." Nicholas's ears actually went red. I was so going to tease him about that later. "I'm not a bloody prince."

"May as well be." Kieran shrugged his good shoulder. "Lady Natasha knows more than half her court would defect if Solange wanted them to. They're just waiting for a better offer."

"I'm still not wearing this." Nicholas plucked at the ribbon on the black velvet sleeve of the doublet

"Yeah, you are," I said cheerfully. "Or else they'll strip you naked when they come get us."

He glared at me for a long time and then pulled off his shirt, muttering vile curses the entire time. I caught a glimpse of bare chest, wondered if I should look away to give him privacy, then decided that it might be my last chance to see him with his shirt off. His arms were lean and sculpted, like a swimmer's.

"I didn't get to see you take your clothes off," he complained.

"That's what you get for sleeping all day," I quipped back. He went farther into the shadows to exchange his pants for the leather breeches. Too bad. When he emerged again, he looked pretty good even though it wasn't his style. And he was lucky there were no tights, after all. He tilted his head.

"You like it."

"Shut up." I blushed. I hated vampire extrasensory perception. It wasn't fair that he could hear my heartbeat or smell my skin or whatever.

"Girls are so weird."

Kieran snorted. "No kidding."

"Please, you two were fighting ten minutes ago, and now you're the best of friends?" I said witheringly. "*Guys* are weird." I turned back to Solange, touched her hand. "She's still not moving."

Nicholas and Kieran both went grim, quiet.

"She'll need blood," Nicholas finally said. "But I'm sure Bruno got hold of my parents by now, and they'll bring it with them. I doubt it's a secret Solange is here. Natasha does rather seem to want to make this as public as possible."

"Do we have a plan?"

"We fight like hell."

"Good plan."

◆

It wasn't long before the Araksaka filed down the stone steps to escort us to the hall. I wouldn't let go of Solange's hand, even when one of them lifted her up to slide an embroidered silver robe over her torn dress. She looked so fragile, with her dark hair and pale features. They marched us upstairs. They wore white silk shirts and heavy breeches, which should have made them look silly but instead made them seem even more fierce. One of them shoved me when I got in the way because I was still clinging to Solange. I stumbled.

"Hey, don't touch my girlfriend." Nicholas seethed.

"Girlfriend?" I blinked at him. He thought of me as his girlfriend? Then I shoved the guard back, before anyone could see me blushing. "I mean, get off of me."

The hall was beautiful, crowded with candles and lanterns hanging from the ceiling and even more mirrors everywhere. Apparently Lady Natasha really liked looking at herself. A long table held countless jugs of every description: silver inlaid with rubies, gold, carved mahogany, painted china. I knew every single one of them held blood. Musicians played in one corner, the soft notes of harp and piano and violin drifting around us.

Lady Natasha's courtiers were easy to recognize—they all wore raven feathers in their hair. The rest kept their allegiances more subtle; I didn't know the meanings behind most of the pendants and embroidered family crests. I didn't see London or anyone else from the Drake family. I did see yards of velvet and silk embroidered with gold thread, brocade gowns, elaborate wigs. I wouldn't have been entirely surprised if Marie Antoinette strolled by. They drifted and lolled and reclined gracefully on chaises and piles of cushions.

Solange was carried up to a dais draped with red sari fabric. In the middle was a glass bier on which she was stretched out. Her hand fell over the side and lay there limply. There were roses all around her. A raven flew down from a crevice in the ceiling and perched patiently at Solange's feet. Another raven landed, and another. Soon she was surrounded by huge black birds, all watching her expectantly. The old-fashioned grandfather clock read nearly midnight. When it rang its twelfth chime Solange would have to wake up then and there.

Or not at all.

"Welcome, welcome," Lady Natasha called from her white throne. We were herded toward her. She wore a white gown with sequined silk over her panniers. Her pale straight hair fell to her elbows, and on her head she wore a medieval horned crown hung with sheer veils that draped to the floor. She dripped diamonds;

they were around her neck, wrists, fingers, and even around her ankles beneath the sway of her bell skirt. Hope sat next to her in an evening gown and high-heeled sandals. And just when I thought it couldn't get much more surreal, Lady Natasha clapped her hands regally.

"Let the celebrations begin."

The crowd broke off into couples in the wide space of the hall, and they whirled in a waltz as the music swelled. They wore medieval dresses, Norse aprons, Tudor whale-boned corsets, Victorian dancing slippers, pin-striped suits from the 1920s, dashing pirate shirts, and velour frock coats. They circled in a kaleidoscope of colors and fabrics until the sheer press of them started to make me dizzy.

Solange lay still; even her chest was frozen, suspended in the bloodchange. Her lips went purple, as if they were bruised. The blue of her veins traced under her parchment skin, like rivers through a winter landscape..

"Her lips are turning blue," I whispered to Nicholas. He nodded grimly.

"She hasn't much time."

I'd never felt so helpless in my life. I could only stand there in the elegant ballroom inside the mountain and watch my best friend struggle not to die. She moved once, jerking as if electricity fired through her. Kieran took one step forward and was roughly shoved backward by one of the guards. Lady Natasha's laugh was light and pretty.

"Soon all this will be over," she said, preening.

"Sooner than you think."

CHAPTER 27

♦

Lucy

We whirled, recognizing the voice. Liam stood in a white cloud, wearing silver nose plugs. He pointed to three guards rushing at him with axes.

"Sleep."

They crumpled, axes clattering to the ground.

Hypnos.

"You," Lady Natasha sneered. "You're too late. Your precious daughter has nearly slipped away completely. My throne is safe, this kingdom is safe."

"Let's see, shall we?" Helena asked, her swords flashing, her black braid hanging neatly down her back. Her sons flooded in behind them, joined by Hart and his agents. I'd never seen so many nose plugs and so much black army gear in my whole life.

The waltzing courtiers turned to a more violent dance. The

music was drowned out by the sounds of swords clashing. The tribes chose their sides, and the Drakes and Helios weren't nearly as outnumbered as I'd feared. The Araksaka convened around Lady Natasha—all but Conan. I did what he'd suggested earlier, and I stayed down. In fact, I crawled on my hands and knees through broken crockery toward the bier. The ravens stayed by Solange, cawing viciously. When one bent his head, about to poke into her eye, I picked up a crystal shard and whipped it at him. He squawked and flew off, offended, in a flurry of feathers. I wished I had my crossbow.

Helena was tumbling like some deranged acrobat, flinging knives and stakes as she went. She left a trail of dust and ash behind her. Helios agents scattered like beetles, blowing Hypnos to clear the vampires out of their way. It was like Sleeping Beauty's castle—ladies in fine dresses and gentlemen in complicated cravats all dropping to the Persian rugs, asleep. Crystal vases tumbled off tables; wooden chairs splintered under impact.

Hart's agents ignored Natasha's courtiers once they fell, preferring to attack Hope's rogue unit. Blood splattered the stones, stained the tapestries.

Liam strode toward the bier, his grim eyes never leaving his fading daughter. He took out three vampires without moving his glance away even once. One of Hope's men flew backward after a vicious punch, face bruising before he even hit the wall.

Nicholas rolled toward me, landing at my elbow. His eyes were fierce. He grabbed my chin and kissed me hard. It was over before I had time to react.

"Stay down," he ordered.

"Duh," I shot back, and returned the kiss, just as quick and just as hard before he dove away to gather stakes from a sleeping guard. He rose from a crouch and threw them like deadly confetti. They all moved so fast, it was like a watercolor painting, all blurs and smears. A woman dressed in red silk bared her fangs and hurled a sleek jet stake. Logan caught it before it imbedded itself in Nicholas's chest.

"Shame to ruin such a nice jacket," he said.

"Took your time getting here," Nicholas returned with a grin, whirling to meet the next advance. They fought back to back like a spinning top of fury.

Helena reached Lady Natasha with a feral grin. Lady Natasha lifted her chin haughtily but stepped behind one of her guards. Helena slashed at his raven tattoos relentlessly until it was just her and the queen. Their swords met, clashing like ice cracking in the sea.

Hart followed Hope down the tunnel when she made a dash for safety. The rest of the battle went on, both impossibly quick and dragging on forever.

I kept crawling around the bodies, ducking flying boots and weapons. I had to get to Solange. I reached the bier with only shallow scrapes and a bruise from the elbow of a clumsy Helios-Ra agent. I swatted at the ravens until they flew off, landing on nearby furniture and eyeing me malevolently. Solange was cold, so cold I snatched my fingers back. Her eyelids and fingertips were the same purple as her lips. She made strange wheezing sounds, as if she was trying to breathe but couldn't. Her mouth opened and closed, like a baby bird starving for its first meal.

And I had nothing to give her.

Which wasn't even our biggest problem.

"Natasha, darling, you always did know how to throw a proper party."

The fighting stopped. It was as if someone pressed a cosmic pause button. Everyone turned to stare at the vampire now standing just inside the cave, surrounded by warriors in brown leather tunics. He was smirking, his pale face striking under long black hair. I'd have thought he'd used Hypnos with the way people were reacting. He walked slowly forward, as if he had all the time in the world. His guard kept pace.

"Montmartre," Lady Natasha murmured, satisfied. "I knew you'd come."

Leander Montmartre and his Host. Lady Natasha was the only one who was pleased with this new development. She actually shook Helena off to smooth her hair back into place. The mirrors reflected her smug, chilling smile.

"Yes, darling, but you're looking a little haggard." His gray eyes tracked Solange's fitful breathing, her bruised-looking lips. "I've come for her, actually."

The smile turned to a snarl. "No."

"Of course." He sniffed the air as if it were laced with perfume. "No one else will do, surely you know that."

"She's a child. You love *me*."

"Love." He flicked a surprisingly smooth manicured hand. I would have expected it to have long nails crusted with blood, that's how menacing his aura was. "Don't be banal."

"You've let yourself be swayed by talk of prophecies and legacies. But I'll change that, you'll see. She's nearly dead."

"I'll have her, Natasha," he said coldly.

"You'll die first," she shot back. "Araksaka!"

At Natasha's command her tattooed guard swarmed forward to attack. She threw a whitethorn stake, fangs gleaming. Montmartre's Host bared their own teeth and leaped into the fray. The snarling and growling made the hair on my arms stand up. Vampires turned to ash all around Montmartre, as if he was standing in a dusty field on a windy day.

"A moment, if you please," he interrupted.

Again, the fighting stopped.

"There's no need to thin our numbers this way," he said pleasantly. "All I want is the girl."

"Stay the hell away from my daughter." Helena seethed. She flung her own stake, but one of the Hounds intercepted it before it could hit its mark.

"Your daughter needs me," Montmartre told her. "So you'd best mind your manners when you speak to me." He held up a chain with a glass vial encrusted with silver ivy leaves. "My Host were tracking in the woods and came across this most curious artifact." Every single one of Solange's brothers hissed. "I am assured this was once filled with Veronique's blood, for Solange here. There are only a few drops left, but it should be enough. It rather looks as if she needs it."

Solange was barely breathing, and she was so pale the blue of her veins made her look nearly violet.

She was dying.

Or about to turn into a *Hel-Blar*.

I wasn't sure which was worse.

"Hang on," I whispered. "Please, please hang on."

"I am prepared to let her have this," Montmartre continued, swinging the chain. The Drakes watched it, as if he were a hypnotist. "But I am going to need something in return."

"What is it you want?" Liam asked, standing close to Helena, his hand on her arm. She was straining not to explode.

"Why, I want the queen, of course."

"I'm the queen," Lady Natasha barked. Montmartre ignored her, which enraged her further. The whites of her eyes were slowly going red.

"You give me Solange, and I will give her life."

"No way," I croaked, though no one paid any attention to me.

Liam suddenly looked old, as if all of his years were hitting him at once. He nodded his head once.

"Dad, no!" Quinn advanced.

"She'll die," Liam said. "She doesn't have any time left. We have no options."

Montmartre gave a courtly bow and strode toward the bier, his Host at his side. Liam was jostled, trying to hold back his family.

"Trust me," he whispered.

I felt sick. Montmartre leaned down and picked Solange's unresponsive body up into his arms.

"No," Liam said furiously. "Now. You give it to her now where we can see."

"I don't recall offering that," he said. Solange looked so tiny against his chest.

"*Now.*"

"Montmartre," a new voice interrupted, sounding young but hard. "Weren't you going to invite us to the wedding?"

The girl looked about my age, but she was a vampire, so she could have been a hundred years old for all I knew. She had long black hair and wore a leather tunic and bone beads in her hair. There were tattoos on her hands and arms.

Cwn Mamau. The Hounds.

The Host snarled. The girl and her warriors snarled back. These were the vampires Montmartre had turned and who had then turned against him. The Host hated the Hounds on sight. Montmartre didn't look too pleased either. And for the first time, he looked faintly disconcerted.

"Isabeau. Go home, little girl."

"The Hounds do not support your claim to the throne," she told him very precisely, her accent French. She nodded a greeting to Liam and Helena. "I apologize for the delay." She turned back to Montmartre. "We will not be ruled by you."

"It hardly matters what you savage whelps want," he said, but his demeanor had changed. Even I could see it. He wasn't quite as confident. Fury and something else I couldn't read colored his movements. He flicked a glance at his Host. "Take her."

Another battle. The Hounds and the Host were evenly matched.

Which was all fine and good except that Solange didn't have this kind of time.

Blood splattered the floor along with the ashes. It was so fast and so feral, I had a hard time keeping track of what was going on. I did see Nicholas creeping forward, staying low. Then he disappeared into a blur and Montmartre's feet went out from under him. Solange tumbled from his grasp, landing half sprawled against the bier.

A Hound smashed his fist into Nicholas's face, then flipped him over two more Host fighting a Hound. He hurtled into a table and then lay still. I cried out.

"Human!" the Hound girl shouted before plucking the vial from the floor and throwing it. It flew toward me, its silver chain catching the light from the candles.

A hand caught it in midair.

Not my hand.

"Are you kidding me?" I screeched. It was Juliana, Natasha's bored sister, who'd flitted around us when we were first captured. She waggled the vial at me. I wanted to claw her eyes right out of her head. I launched myself at her. What I lacked in finesse I made up for with angry flailing and a stubborn need for vengeance. I was not going to lose Solange. Not again and not when her cure was so close.

I was no match for Juliana unfortunately. That was clear after the first punch to my face. The second I ducked, but I wasn't quick enough to avoid the third one, to my stomach. I staggered, nauseous and breathless. The vial swung tauntingly in front of me. I grabbed for it and missed.

And then Kieran was suddenly there, swinging with his good arm. The vial dropped next to his boot. Juliana reached for it and

I kicked her hard, right in the throat. She swung up snarling, fangs extended. Kieran was closer to the vial and couldn't fight her off with his broken arm.

"Go," I yelled at him. "Go, go, go."

He grabbed the vial and skidded to Solange's side just as I crashed into a delicate chair that had the good grace to break apart on impact. One of the legs, painted with pink rosebuds, broke off. At least I had a weapon now.

"I'm going to kill you, little girl!" Juliana yelled.

The chair leg didn't quite pierce her heart, but it was near enough to make her freeze, gasp, and clutch at her chest.

"Lucy!" The stake Nicholas tossed at me finished her off. Ash drifted at my feet, like mist. My first vampire kill. When I got home, I'd have to recite countless malas to appease my mother. And my churning stomach. But not right now; right now I could indulge in a moment of triumph. But only a moment.

Because it was just one of those days.

I hung over the back of a bench, trying to convince my severely bruised diaphragm that standing up really was a necessity. Kieran leaned over Solange, tipping the contents of the silver vial between her lips. Those precious drops ran down into her throat. Still, she didn't look particularly healed.

"Nicholas," I croaked. "It's not working."

He ducked a dagger with a rusted handle. "It stopped the sickness, but now she needs to feed." He threw an entire stool at an approaching Araksaka guard. "She needs human blood—it's better for the first time."

I was trying to drag myself over to the bier, but Kieran was already slicing a shallow cut across his forearm. He held it to Solange's mouth, urging her to drink, whispering.

"Drink," he begged her. "I can't lose you now, not after all this. Drink, damn it." For some reason, the way he spoke to her, gently and desperately, had tears burning on my cheeks.

Lady Natasha howled, her long pale hair flying behind her like a banner. Her dress was stained with blood. Several of the carved ravens on her throne had broken off. "Montmartre! You love me," she howled, even as she tried to fight off Helena.

Montmartre's Host weren't exactly losing the fight with the Hounds, but they weren't winning it either. Hunters, vampire rogues, half the royal court under Conan's direction, and the Drake family all stood against them. Montmartre cursed.

"Fall back," he ordered. The Host retreated instantly to form a circle around him. "She will be my queen," Montmartre promised before flicking his hand. The Host pressed against him and they retreated down one of the tunnels.

Lady Natasha, abandoned on all sides, turned her anger to Helena. Helena twirled a stake until she found a proper grip. The fight stretched on, two determined women with a penchant for ancient weaponry. It was a beautiful dance, in its way, flashing blades and flips through the air. But in the end, Helena's stake flew true. Lady Natasha blinked uncomprehendingly and then her empty dress fell in a delicate heap of fine silk, dusted with ash.

The noise and fury in the hall stopped so suddenly, it practically echoed. Even the Araksaka paused.

Each to a one, the vampires dropped to one knee in front of Helena.

In lieu of rightful succession, killing the present monarch granted you the crown.

Nicholas limped up beside me and held on to my hand tightly. I squeezed his fingers, stepping back so that our sides were pressed together, feeling better with his cool skin against mine. Neither of us spoke. We didn't have to.

On the glass bier, Solange finally gasped once, then swallowed hungrily. When she opened her eyes and saw dozens of kneeling vampires in their best court finery, she groaned weakly, blood smeared on her lips.

"Oh God, I'm not a vampire queen, am I?"

EPILOGUE

◆

Solange

I met Lucy in town. She was determined to force me into a semblance of a normal life, and meeting for coffee every Thursday night was her current plan. She was waiting for me in the park. It hadn't even been a week since I'd turned, and I wasn't ready to face the temptation of a coffeehouse full of human hearts beating all around me. I could ignore the squirrels and the fox hiding in the far bushes.

Lucy was sitting on a bench with two paper cups and a plastic to-go container filled with what was left of a chocolate-covered cherry tart. She wiped crumbs off her hands.

"I'm still celebrating," she mumbled through a mouthful. "I won't be able to fit into my clothes if I keep this up." She eyed me critically. "You're wearing that?"

I frowned at my clay-stained pants. "So? I didn't know I had to dress up for you."

She eyed me again. "How are you feeling?"

"I'm *fine*. You're as bad as my brothers." I felt better than fine, actually. I felt strong and alert, my eyes amplified every spark of light from the moon, the stars, streetlights. It was a little distracting, I had to admit, to hear her heart beating and smell the warmth of her blood just under her skin. And disconcerting to know my brothers had been right: blood now tasted better than chocolate. In fact, I couldn't remember much from the night of the caves, just the taste of Kieran in my mouth. He'd left with his uncle before I could properly thank him.

"Any word from Kieran?" Lucy asked quietly as if she'd known I was thinking about him.

I shook my head, tried not to look like I cared. I had enough to occupy me, after all. My mom was the new queen, which meant the prophecy hadn't technically been fulfilled. We weren't sure what to think about that. And we were still replacing an entire wall of the farmhouse, which had been burned out by Hope's unit. The gardens were full of water and soot. Bruno needed stitches, and Hyacinth wouldn't leave her room or lift the black lace veil off her face. London disappeared down the tunnels again; no one knew to where. And I'd actually caught Nicholas sending roses to Lucy's house, and they were on the phone with each other all the time.

And Montmartre was still out there. He'd sent an engagement gift: a diamond ring.

I'd flushed it down the toilet.

So I was too busy to sit around thinking about Kieran Black.

"Oh, here." Lucy passed me a package tied with ribbon. "A

belated birthday present from my dad." She rolled her eyes when I pulled out a piece of carved deer antler on a leather tong. "When he heard about the deer heart, he said to tell you the deer is clearly your totem animal and should be honored."

I slipped it over my head as she guzzled the rest of her drink. Her eyes watered.

"Ouch, still hot." She stood up quickly.

I stared at her. "Where are you going? I just got here."

She grinned at me, her gaze flicking toward the sidewalk.

"You have a date."

I froze.

"Lucy Hamilton, what have you done?"

"Gotta go!" She darted out of the park before I could say anything else. I didn't have to look to know who it was standing there. I could smell him, taste him.

Kieran.

"Solange," he said softly. He looked good, even with the bruises on his jaw going yellow and the sling cradling his arm. He didn't smile, but the way he was looking at me made me feel warm all over. I stood up.

"Kieran." I didn't know what else to say.

So I leaned over and kissed him.

ALYXANDRA HARVEY studied creative writing and literature at York University and has had her poetry published in magazines. She likes lattes, chocolate, and tattoos and lives in an old Victorian farmhouse in Ontario, Canada, with her husband and three dogs.

www.alyxandraharvey.com
www.thedrakechronicles.com

Don't miss the next installment in the
Drake Chronicles, coming soon!

BLOOD
FEUD

by

ALYXANDRA HARVEY